The Predecessor

M.R Browne

Published by Clink Street Publishing 2021

Copyright © 2021

First edition.

ISBN: 978-1-914498-99-2

To Tom – wherever you are

Chapter One

It was a glum April afternoon when first I saw him.

Parliament had gone into recess early and, with an eye to a press release about working through my Easter, I had headed back to my constituency, where holidays go to die.

Lunch with a party donor (lamb undercooked, gratitude overdone), conspicuously local pint drunk in the town Wetherspoons, five advice surgery appointments ground through. It was the usual fare – housing waiting list delays, benefit screw-ups and one gripe about excessive disabled parking spaces at Sainsbury's.

Unusually, I was facing the hopes, fears and cock-eyed resentments of my constituents alone. My caseworker, Adam, had a cold and – stretching my good boss routine to its utmost – I had advised him to stay in bed with a Lemsip. With Machiavellian cunning, Adam had moved in with a journalist in the local newspaper a few months back. My resultant terror of leaks had shifted the power balance between us and transformed his leave allowance.

Defenceless against my electorate, I sat alone in my office, waiting for my next surgery appointment.

There was a blur of movement behind the glass door. Next customer please.

'Come in.'

The shadow stayed still.

'The door is open, come in.'

Still the shadow did not move. I had a sense of being watched.

Lazy sod. I got up to open the door myself.

The corridor stretched before me. White walls, blue carpet – nobody standing on it.

I took a few paces and peered into the empty office next door. Empty. I took a few more, and inspected the kitchen area. Only tea stains greeted me.

Confused, I headed back to the office. Definitely no one there.

Just as I reached the door again a scent drifted across me. Rich, nicotine-y, but not the grey tang of cigarettes. Something darker, deeper. A flashed memory of a grandfather. Pipe smoke.

I looked around again. Still nothing.

First signs of a stroke? Unexplained smells, strange visions, the senses acting up. Brain disease. Working too hard. I was definitely working too hard. I sat in the best office chair and composed obituaries:

'a martyr to his electorate', 'worked himself to the bone', 'a rare example of a committed constituency MP, tragically too committed'.

The phone rang through my daydreams. The deferential old dear on the other end was suitably impressed that her MP had picked up his own office phone. She burbled apologies, saying she would have to cancel her surgery appointment as her dog had eaten a frog and was worried it could be 'one of those foreign, poisonous ones'. I was all graciousness, especially when I realised she was to have been my last appointment.

I locked and left the office – the smell of pipe tobacco had entirely gone. I puzzled over it all the way to Waitrose, until the challenge of buying a pizza and some Imodium without any of my constituents recognising me put the matter entirely out of my mind.

That day, that first day I saw him, was two years into my first term. Two arid, sexless, wasted years as Member of Parliament for Holton.

A bog-standard, eminently overlookable MP, for a bog-standard, eminently overlookable place.

The Parliamentary constituency of Holton is shaped like a disgusting parsnip.

At its wide base lie the suburbs of Bristol's suburbs. Two straggling, pebble-dashed, diesel-scoured settlements, known as Netley and Pilford, where medium-income Bristolian couples go to spawn, bicker and grow fat together. The two suburbs, nothing more than a collection of identikit housing developments, failing industrial estates and arterial roads, have pretensions towards an identity more meaningful than their dreary reality – the grey, chewy fat at the scrag end of a provincial city. Like exiled Russian aristocrats, they pine for the past – the distant, hay-scented days when Netley and Pilford were sleepy hamlets in rural Gloucestershire, replete with benevolent squires and amorous parsons, before the city set them in concrete from the feet up.

Residents' associations fetishistically adorn fragments of old farm buildings with heritage plaques, refer to scrappy little municipal parks as meadows and banish any local reference to North Bristol (or, heaven forbid, Avon). There is even a local Cultural Preservation Society, frantically looking for anything to preserve beyond pubs built to show Sky Sports, supermarket car parks and the West of England's largest Sofa Warehouse. At the borders of Netley, the larger of the brick-bloated suburbs, a sign reads 'Welcome to Netley, a historic Gloucestershire Town'. I laugh every time I pass it. I am from Netley.

Much of this inferiority complex comes from the genuine countryside to the north of Netley and Pilford that makes up the rest of the constituency. Past the outermost arterial road, a tapering finger of green curves up into real Gloucestershire, taking in acres of prime grazing land, a handful of pretty villages and two stately homes. The arc of tourism directs its stream to the south of Bristol (drawn towards slutty Bath, then deep into the tarted-up West Country), leaving this countryside fairly unspoilt. Here, locals still show champion ferrets in pubs that don't do food, the sons and daughters of minor gentry host drug parties in ancient hunting lodges and farmers mistreat their animals. The landscape is beautiful, but firmly privately owned – on the few footpaths that do cross the woods and fields, stray walkers are liable to be shot at by red-faced men whose livings are derived from slaughtering anything soft, fluffy and capable of movement.

Attached to this parsnip shaft of merry old England – like a tumour budding from its tip – bulges Holton itself. It is what a Netley and Pilford long to be: a genuine English Market Town. Deep in history, rich in architectural detail and as rigidly, cruelly hierarchical as an Ottoman Court. The town is ruled by an elite – cords wearing, Sunday paper reading, monogamy pretending. These worthies draw their power from Holton's institutions – the grammar school, the minster church, the town council – on which they sit, lords of all committees and all creation. Together they perch, in an endless round of boardrooms and dinner parties, and plot how to build Holton's walls yet higher, the only place for 20 miles around with a theatre, a Waitrose and no new housing.

Farmers still head loyally into Holton every month for the livestock fair, where local poachers sell pheasants and home-imported tobacco for a fiver in the marketplace, just as they have done for generations. Famers and poachers alike take their wives for dinner in one of the town's Italian restaurants (independent of course. Chains are banned from the town, on pain of social death), before availing themselves of a pint from the iconic 'Holton Hare' brewery pub (subsidised directly and indirectly by the town council). The Holton Valley Hunt still meet outside the pub every Boxing Day, allowing people who seek emotional and sexual satisfaction from sweat and blood-drenched dealings with the animal kingdom to associate freely. Holton Police officers, members of the Mid Gloucs Temple to a man, turn a blind eye to most animal welfare laws (part of a local judicial distrust of anything that reached the statute book after 1963).

It is the snobs in Holton who I have to thank for my election. The town has voted quietly, discreetly, relentlessly Tory for centuries. Similar towns of the rural intelligentsia (leatherbound Isherwood in the study, Turkish cookbooks by the AGA, wife swapping in the Jag) tend to lean towards Liberal Democrat, but not Holton. The Whigs removed one of the town's two MPs in the Great Reform Act and, nearly 200 years on, Holton still hasn't forgiven the Party's descendants for the insult. Every General Election, a hustings takes place in the Town Council Hall, where the good people of the town gather to stare icily at the Labour and Liberal candidates ('all the same, don't trust the buggers'), and to clap politely at the Tory. Once, when a young Thatcherite sang a hymn to rising house prices in the area, they actually cheered – the only spontaneous outburst of public emotion ever recorded in Holton. Come polling day, no posters go up, no rosettes grace the Georgian streets, but convoys of waxed cars glide gracefully to the polling station, to deposit cross after cross in the Tory box.

The problem for Holton is that usually this isn't enough. The farming belt votes Tory of course, a traditional rabbit placed in tribute at the squire's door – but the iron law of constituency boundaries is against them. The gin-and-tonic-swilling bores of the town and the blood-guzzling maniacs of the country may stand together in the Tory interest, but against the raw numbers of the suburbs this counts for naught. Holton gives the constituency its name, but Pilford and Netley provide most of the voters.

This is deliberate. In the 1960s, as Britain basked in the white heat of technological and social revolution and new suburbs sprang up like weeds, Harold Wilson and his government looked for opportunities to infest Tory seats with new voters. The growth of Bristol made Holton a clear target – and the new suburbs of Netley and Pilford were promptly tacked onto the south of the constituency. Demographics did the rest, and within a few years the majority of Holton voters lived in pebble-dashed houses, went on package holidays and voted for the Labour politicians ushering in the new age of affordable delight. Even when the consumer revolution fizzled out in the dingy light of the 70s, they loyally kept voting Labour.

No more were the bewhiskered sons of Gloucestershire gentry returned as Tory voting fodder; instead a teacher named Alan, then a social scientist called Jean, sat to represent Netley and Pilford, and to drive Holton into a fury. In the General Election of 1987 that rage reached such a level that Holton town achieved a 95% turnout, as every good Waitrose shopper came out to sock it to the lower middle classes who had the insolence to keep imposing on their betters. This unprecedented turnout in the north, combined with a few of the suburbanites in the south falling for the animal magnetism of Thatcherism in its highest pomp, saw a Tory scrape in for the first time in 20 years. The aberration was corrected five years later, aided by the new MP's coke addiction, and Labour returned to whisper in the ear of Holton town that it too was mortal.

This was my immediate predecessor, Dr Duncan Middleton. A local GP and young Labour Cllr in Pilford, he retook the seat in 1992 and seemed to have claimed it forever for Labour in 1997, when his majority reached 12,000. In that golden May for the left, even a few of the great and good of Holton were rumoured to have voted for that nice Mr Blair, assured that with him their house prices and sweeping rural views were safe. In the 13 years that followed, the glow in Dr Middleton's cheeks receded with every Blairite deal with the devil, until at last in 2010 he appeared as a walking ghost from an age long since passed. A man of new, sunlit dawns seemed ill suited to the grizzle, grind and grubbiness of the second decade of the 21st century. His evident tiredness, combined with voters in Netley and Pilford reaching new heights in their desire to emulate their rural neighbours and betters, saw my narrow election (majority of 679) as Conservative Member for Holton.

Dr Middleton died the year after I defeated him. On paper it was a brain tumour; according to his widow it was the final widening of the crack in his heart from the day he voted for the Iraq War. I went to the funeral, suppressed inappropriate thoughts about his teenage daughters and played the dutiful public servant honouring a fallen comrade. Et in arcadia ego.

That's the Holton constituency, the place I blame for my failure to be promoted after two years of sweating on the Conservative backbenches. MPs for interesting constituencies get noticed, get given interesting jobs. MPs like me, for everyday places, get forgotten; left to host advice surgeries on their own on cold Friday evenings – and to be the subject of a haunting.

Chapter Two

At Westminster, it is always the first day of school. The big kids run around the place, proud of owning it. Little kids like me, wearing shiny new clothes and a look of always being lost, get barged in corridors and viciously towel whipped in the showers.

Ministers in particular seem to enjoy getting names wrong. In my first two years I have been called 'Young Mr Wilkins' (by the Minister for Farming), 'John' (the Chief Whip) and 'Wang' (a tired and emotional Health Secretary). My name is Robert Wilkes. I briefly double barrelled my surname, using my mother's name of Vernon, until a Party grandee told me that it was vulgar. I pulped the last of the 'Mr Robert Vernon-Wilkes MP Esq' headed notepaper and returned to plain old Wilkes.

It has been another long day of not getting noticed in Parliament. I had bopped up and down in Education questions, desperate to ask the Schools Minister about increased spending in my constituency, the wisdom of his policy and the greatness of his mind. The Speaker, as usual, didn't notice. After popping out for a despairing wee, one of the terrifying stewards of the House, all black pantaloons, beard and 800 years of authority, stopped me from re-entering, saying 'MPs only, sir'. Once again, I had been taken for an intern. He raised one eyebrow as he looked at my hastily proffered pass and let me in with a grunt.

I gave up on bobbing back and forth when hunger pangs grew too strong, retreating to one of the cafés in Portcullis House to slurp at some soup. I was on my own and grew convinced that the table of researchers next door were laughing at me. They were all young and horribly virile. One of them was a blonde girl, all 20 years old and sparkling eyes. As I tried to sneak a discreet glance at her, I spilt soup all down my front. The girl got up to offer a fistful of napkins, 'so you can dry yourself off, sir'.

I fled to my office, squirrelled away at the furthest end of the Parliamentary estate. Only June was in. June has worked in Westminster for 30 years and is on better terms with most senior ministers than I am. She wears cardigans from Marks & Spencer and can reply to letters at a rate of six an hour. June disapproves of me. Having worked in Downing Street in the 1980s, run a leadership bid in the 90s and worked steadily through the long years of Conservative opposition, I am but a blip on her CV, a boring prelude to full retirement.

'Hi June, just thought I would pop up to see how you are getting on.'

'Fine thank you, Robert. Your shirt is stained.'

'Ah, yes. Soup. Don't think anyone will notice when it dries though.'

June did not dignify my statement with a reply.

I sat in the armchair and checked my emails on my phone. After five minutes, I could tell from June's sharp little breaths that she assumed I was playing Candy Crush. The tension was too much.

'Better get going, June. Keep up the good work.'

'Goodbye, Robert.'

I ended up sitting in the gent's toilet for two hours. A safe place. Such is power.

I left when someone occupied the stall next to me, driven by the paranoid fear that they might recognise me from my shoes (John Lewis and scuffed).

I went to Westminster Hall to try to look useful. For those not familiar with the Palace, Westminster Hall is the oldest part of Parliament. Unlike the rest, it is authentically medieval. Here there is no overdone, overheated neo-gothic gilt; here there is no heavy, decadent carpet – here is only bare grey stone. The gossip-, sweat- and stale tea-infused fog of the rest of the Palace is centuries away. The air in the Hall is cold, jagged, sharp. The Hall's historic use has been twofold: as a courtroom for treason trials and as a resting place for the bodies of the great and good. The smell of the judicial axe and the royal embalming fluid lingers.

To one side of the Hall is a smaller room, stuffed with chairs. In here, Westminster Hall debates take place. Backbench MPs can secure these fairly easily, and junior ministers are sent over to bat for the government. MPs and Ministers alike always seem faintly uncomfortable in these debates, unsettled perhaps by the medieval setting and ghosts from Westminster's savage past, mocking their warm lattes and soft round bottoms.

The sheer pointlessness of the proceedings adds a further grimness. New MPs, keen to impress their constituents, wait for months to be allocated a Westminster Hall debate. Once the long-coveted slot is acquired, they spend weeks imploring colleagues and journalists to attend, and burn the midnight oil trying to channel JFK or Churchill (choose according to political taste) into their speech on the urgent need to save the Northampton to Kettering 938 Sunday bus service. On the day, they give the speech to a bored minister, a loyal researcher – and if they are very lucky, an MP from an opposing party out to score some political points. All present agree that Northampton and Kettering are fine towns, and that buses are, generally speaking, good things. The opposing MP lays into the proposing MP's party for letting buses everywhere down. The Minister reads out lines written by a civil servant committing the government to continue acknowledging the reality of buses. The loyal researcher fires off a press release proclaiming progress towards saving a vital bus link. Then everyone goes home. The press release goes unread, and the 938 service is scrapped a week later.

I have never yet managed to secure a Westminster Hall debate.

That day, my colleague Tony Wellington had – on fuel duty. Tony's constituency was 20 miles north of mine, a southern colony of the West Midlands, replete with closed car-making factory and a stout named after it. Tony had got elected at the same time as me, also overturning a Labour majority – but with a far bigger swing. The bastard had won the seat on the slogan of 'Give Westminster some Welly', and had promptly cornered the Westminster market in presenting as the hard-on-taxes, soft-on-racism face of blue-collar Conservatism. He had already achieved 'rising star' status, being profiled by the Sun and lauded by a number of libertarian-aligned think tanks. Today's debate, calling for a further cut in fuel duty, was the latest phase of his crusade to give taxation the death by a thousand cuts.

I walked on just as he was describing Britain's drivers as 'like their ancestors in the trenches – plucky Tommies, ploughing through swamps of red tape and enduring bombardment after bombardment from distant taxmen. Heroes, fighting to grow our economy, sustained only by the hope of better days and the homely comforts of a Greggs sausage roll'. I turned my gag into a growl of comradely acclamation and sat down, next to a bored Welsh Nationalist.

Tony ploughed on for some time, a mounting erection

visible through his Savile Row trousers. As he sat, his researcher, seated a few rows behind, clapped. The claps echoed through the grey, silent room like gunshots. The Labour Transport Spokesperson rose, to welcome the sentiments expressed and to remind Tony that benefit cuts, imposed by the government he supported, represented a still greater assault on the cost of living of the poorest. Tony chuntered in his seat. The Welsh Nationalist snored in his. The final player in the drama, the Minister – all sensible blouse and quirky glasses – rose to respond for the government. She thanked Tony for all his campaigning and highlighted that the government was committed to a 'new renaissance of the roads'.

I saw my chance to raise a constituency issue and get a line in Hansard. Maybe this afternoon wasn't wasted. I rose and the Minster bowed her head, allowing my intervention.

'Would my honourable friend assure me that the government's excellent road plan concentrates on sensible, achievable road plans – and does not include the proposed M17a route? This roadway would devastate hundreds of acres of pristine countryside in my constituency, without alleviating Bristol to Worcester congestion.'

Feeling pleased, I planned my press release. The Minister replied:

'I thank the honourable gentleman for his intervention, which is noted. To return to the main point of discussion, we have to put the case for further fuel duty cuts in the context of the very serious financial situation that the last Labour government left us. A broken government, with broken ideas, broke our economy and…'

She droned on, and I sat, as if slapped. In Parliamentary terms, I had been. The use of honourable gentleman as opposed to honourable friend suggested that the Minister didn't know my name, or party. The use of the dread phrase 'noted' confirmed that I, and any issue I raised, was beneath contempt – to be filed away with complaints about chemtrails and requests for dog poo to be white again.

I had to stick the debate out. Leaving early would be akin to flouncing out of a party after being rejected for a snog. I had flounced out of enough parties to know not to do that. I pretended to scribble in my notepad. Five doodles later and it was over. Tony gave me a sympathetic nod as he headed out. Tosser.

I gave up on the day and went to the pub. The Red Lion sits outside the back entrance of Parliament and serves as the school bike sheds. MPs go there to smoke, drink and put their hands on knees they shouldn't. Journalists go there too, but there is an unspoken agreement that what is said and done in the Lion stays there. Hacks get to keep perfecting their lines in the gents, and MPs in dark corners get to keep on building meaningful connections with young people. Turn and face the wall my darling, as the gentlemen go by.

I ordered a large gin and tonic from one of the inscrutable, unshockable staff members and sat under a dusty bust of David Lloyd George.

Harry Crowhurst was at the next table, alone but for three empty glasses. Twenty years ago, Harry had been a bright young thing – safe seat, family money, junior minister for the arts. He was the most exciting of the young bloods, coasting from Putney to Pimlico on a tide of charm, topped up with champagne.

As the years went on, the champagne corroded the charm. The charismatic energy that had sustained Harry's glittering dance had withered, until it was only enough to sustain a slow, repetitive shamble. The moves that had wowed parties, debating clubs and debutantes had become a grotesque parody of their earlier selves. The hotel suites he had once hired when romance beckoned were now retained for when he couldn't remember the way home. He still occasionally showed up in debates, still wearing the bright ties and light suits of two decades ago, and everyone would pretend that the buttons hadn't rusted and that the cologne on his neck hadn't soured. Alcohol had stuck Harry, as a glued branch sticks a songbird.

Harry nodded to me and tried to say something witty about the weather. I said 'absolutely' – a failsafe political word, providing affirmation without commitment – and pretended to be busy with emails. I was halfway down the Daily Mail website when I felt a shadow over my phone. Assuming Harry had brought himself over to me, I resigned myself to his whiskey breath and slurred conversation and looked up.

It was not Harry. The man who sat next to me had a waistcoat, a white moustache and piercing blue eyes.

'Hello, can I help you?'

The man said nothing, but kept on looking at me, right through me it seemed. I grew concerned – could he be one of my odder constituents? Come to Westminster to wreak revenge for my lack of response to his fourth letter proving that the BBC were broadcasting subversive codes to turn everyone gay? He looked like an old golf club buffer – just the type.

'Look, if you want a surgery appointment, you need to speak to my office. I am a bit busy today.'

The blue eyes twinkled. He growled, 'Going to take you in hand, boy.'

Then he vanished.

I shook my head, vigorously. I closed and opened my eyes. Nobody there.

'Harry, did you see that man?'

Bleary eyes looked up from a bleared cup. 'What man, old bean? Not the tax man I hope!'

Wheezy laughter. And then, more sharply, 'I say, old bean. You can't smoke in here you know. They'll chuck you out. Chuck you out for anything these days.'

It was then I smelt it. Again. Pipe smoke.

I said goodbye to Harry, stumbled across Westminster Bridge to my tiny London flat, and took a sleeping pill. I dreamt of skeletons.

Chapter Three

I woke up 14 hours later, to a headache, two missed calls from June and a follow-up text: 'I think you are in a pub with no signal Robert. Latest casework batch needs signing. Can you swing by the office ASAP? Thanks J'. I will swing by your fucking neck, June.

A sunny spring morning groped its way past the blinds. The flat was a mess. A used tissue perched on a used pizza box, which only partially covered a tabletop scattering of fine white dust. It helps me get through my Parliamentary papers. And through repeat documentaries on the History Channel.

My wardrobe was at the dry cleaners. I went to put on yesterday's suit (crumpled next to an overflowing ashtray) but stopped as my hand touched sweat-greased trouser. The vanished man. Shit.

Tea in a mug that still tasted of microwaved peas. Shave with a blunted razor. Window stare at the traffic and pigeon-shit stain. Still there. Still happened.

I found one cleanish pair of chinos and drenched a shirt in deodorant and shivered my way across Westminster Bridge back into Parliament. Once a week I like to go in extra early, to beat June to the office. I vary the day, to keep her guessing. The office was empty, filled with the sour sweet scent of yesterday's coffee. I rummaged through the paperwork on June's desk for anything interesting and moved the bottom document (a complaint about June failing to invite a local councillor to a Holton sewage action group meeting) to the top, scrawling a large question mark and a 'we need to talk about this grave mistake' on it. After licking her apple and swapping out her desk chair for the broken one, I settled into my armchair to await her arrival.

The door opened with a creak five minutes later, to legs a lot nicer than June's. 'Oh, good morning, sir. You are in bright and early.'

'Hello, are you, um, feeling better?'

'I was on holiday, sir.'

'Jolly good. Nice to see you back, Rachel.'

Rachel. Lovely Rachel. Twenty-two years old, hard working, fresh out of an English degree at a redbrick. I worked hard to focus on these qualities, not the mane of chestnut hair, two-buttons-open blouses and insistence on calling me sir. I may be a mess, but I am not a cliché.

In line with our professional, pleasant relationship, I asked where she had been on her holiday, not which tousle-haired, rugby-playing, public-school gimp she had gone with.

'Croatia, getting some early sun. Also went to a great festival – two days non-stop on the beach.'

Visions of naked bodies writhing on hot sand, blue laser beams pulsing on tanned skin. Mouths opening for pills, closing on painted lips.

No, Robert.

'Sounds great. You haven't missed much here.'

Rachel settled into her desk and turned her computer on. I pretended to leaf through some Select Committee papers. The tap of fingers answering emails filled the office.

'Hope June hasn't left you with too much to return

to.' June was Rachel's line manager and I encouraged backstabbing.

'Oh no, sir, all manageable.' Rachel tended to be frustratingly loyal.

I kept my disappointment internal. Investigating a genuine bullying accusation against June would be a joy – I would be all furrowed brow, respectful reference to high Parliamentary ethical standards and firm but fair sanctions. At the end of it I would keep June on, but in a humiliatingly lowly capacity – demoted from Chief of Staff to Diary Assistant. Maybe even Junior Secretary, with a contractual requirement to attend weekly spelling and grammar training sessions.

I pushed the daydream away. It could never happen. June would simply pick up the phone to one of the three Ministers she had on her CV (and round to dinner at hers on a regular basis) and I would be facing my own disciplinary investigation. Conducted by a government whip, with a sadistic kink and a soundproofed investigation chamber.

I am to power as Luxembourg's army is to NATO.

Tapping filled the air again as Rachel ploughed through her inbox. I decided to go for it.

'Rachel, do you believe in ghosts?'

'Ghosts? Why?'

'Umm, just a silly question a journalist asked me the other day. Just wondering what I should have said.'

A troubled look crossed Rachel's face. She knows that journalists don't speak to me, about anything.

'Umn. That's weird.'

'I know – bloody freaks at the Avon Herald. What do you think though?'

'Umn, well I used to, I suppose, as a child. When I was nine I thought there was a ghost in my room. Used to make horrible scratching noises, all along the walls. Mum didn't believe me. Then there was a horrible smell and Dad had to take the wainscoting up. There was a dead squirrel there. Must have got trapped, poor thing. Not a ghost.'

I laughed and thought of Rachel's childhood home. Too posh for rats, only squirrels allowed. Roast in the AGA, Sunday Times in the study, pony club trophies above the bed.

'Do you still go back often?' Visions of long legs struggling to fit into the childhood bed, boyfriends smuggled in under pink John Lewis Sheets. No, Robert. No.

'Home, you mean? Yeah, lots – especially after Dad's accident.'

I struggled to recall the details. Lawnmower? Golf? Could you injure yourself through golf? It was something to do with grass. I settled for a sympathetic noise.

The phone rang and Rachel answered. I could tell from her long silences, punctuated by professional noises of non-committal acknowledgement, that it was one of the ranters. After five minutes precisely, she said she had another meeting but would pass on the message to Robert right away. She put the phone down with a click and finished her doodle.

'Mr Bradshaw says there is another German General living in Little Kingsley. Waffen SS apparently, now on the Parish Council. I said I would pass it on.'

'Thank you, Rachel.'

'Sir, I was thinking just now, on the ghosts front. There aren't any ghost stories about Parliament. It's a bit funny that, isn't it? I mean, it's so old, and so many things have happened here. There don't seem to be any ladies in white, or ghostly noises or anything. Why is that?'

'Yeah, that is interesting. We should look into this, Rachel – you and me. Bit of a project! Could get an article in the House Magazine about it perhaps.'

Rachel's eyes lit up. She was smart enough to have worked out that the best way of rising up the Parliamentary ladder and escaping ranting phone calls was to get your name on some written work. 'Sounds great, I can defo make some space to help with that.'

'Excellent. I might pop down to the library, start digging around. Do you want to see what you can find online?'

A beaming yes. The office hummed with mutual benevolence.

Then June walked in and fucked it. She shot me a frosty stare.

'Tube problems, June? Never mind, these things happen.' It was 9.03 am.

'Good to see you are ok, Robert. I was worried when I couldn't reach you yesterday. Would you like a paracetamol?'

I pretended to be busy on my phone as she loudly opened the window, muttering about gin fumes. Her broken chair gave a satisfying creak as she sat on it, the seat sinking towards the ground, until only her head and chest were visible above the desk.

'Oh, bad luck. You have broken your chair again.'

June picked up the green and gold fountain pen given to her by a former boss who was now a Cabinet minister and flourished it meaningfully. I had gone far enough.

'Did you say there was some casework that needed signing, June?'

'Yes, give me a minute.'

She was five minutes. Five minutes of paper rustling, frowning at her computer and of Rachel making her a cup of tea. She beckoned me over to her desk when she was ready. No tea for Robert.

The pile of letters was as thick as my hand. Parliamentary casework is the last refuge of deference in Britain.

Constituents with issues write to their MPs when they have nowhere else left to turn. Damp walls, overcharged phone bills, neighbours who smoke weed – all end up in the last chance parliamentary saloon. The MP, like some squirearchial postman, then pings the problem on to people with the actual power to solve it.

Amazingly, it works. The addition of a Parliamentary portcullis to the head of a letter, the squiggle of a member's signature, the rich cream of a postage-paid Parliamentary envelope – an act of transubstantiation. The most ludicrous, most minor of issues are transformed by Parliamentary pixie dust into grave and pressing matters of state – and voila, Mr Curtis can build an extension to house his county-leading collection of Victorian erotica.[1]

That day's offerings were standard. Animal neglect charges to be dismissed (cows enjoy the cold), full refund on a new conservatory (the colour was wrong), Cynthia Durbridge-Vole to get into Holton Grammar (exam marked by a fool), etc., etc., etc. My signature got progressively wilder as I got further down the pile.

We moved on to replies. The way minor functionaries, of both councils and large companies, piss themselves on receipt of a Parliamentary letter never fails to amuse me. I ticked each reply, to signify that it could be accepted and sent on to the constituent. I noted that June had chalked up a lot of wins.

There was one refusal to act as I demanded – on a request for a council house, from an old market trader on his uppers. I felt a twinge of sympathy.

'This one, June – Mr Hogsben. Seems a bit disappointing. Anything more we can do?'

'The waiting list is very long. Plus, I spoke to the housing

---

1 Poor Mr Curtis. Extension built, he opened his 'Netherton museum of the naughty' to the public a year later. They put him on the register.

officer for some background, and it appears [a frown as cold as the Marks & Spencer freezer section] – he drinks.'

She wielded her ministerial pen. I cowered and ticked the reply. Case closed, house refused.

At the bottom of the pile was a final letter, with a blue sticky note grafted to it for prominence, emblazoned with the letter M.

M was code in my office for maternity unit. My re-election was predicated on achieving a negative (stopping the new M17a route) and a positive (hauling in a new maternity unit for Netley Hospital). Since an Ann Summers had opened in Pilford, birth rates had shot up across the region. A new maternity unit was needed, promised in principle by the Department for Health, but as yet not geographically pinned down. It was between Gloucester and Netley.

Gloucester was clearly going to win. Gloucester could be reached in 20 minutes by car by 80% of the fertile population of the heart of the West Region. Gloucester had a hospital with land ready to build on. Gloucester had an MP long in the tooth and old in cunning. Sir Roger Mapehurst had been a backbencher for 30 years, knew every trick in the book and had a junior health minister as a son-in-law. Gloucester was going to get the maternity unit, the breeding population of Netley was to be disappointed, and I was to be a failure.

I struggled against the dying of the light, lobbying, cajoling, glad-handing. The blue sticky note letter was my latest attempt – a missive to the Secretary of State for Health, bringing to his attention a new study (conducted by the dodgiest of Bristol's consulting firms), showing that Netley Hospital had the most sustainable transport links of any hospital in the region. The letter, a masterpiece of drafting, presented this news in glowing terms, asked for a meeting to discuss how this attribute could be used for the proposed new maternity unit, and skated over the question of how women in the early stages of labour were to use cycling lanes to reach hospital.

I signed with an extra bouncy squiggle. 'Excellent letter – I presume Rachel did this one?' June pouted.

'Remember to post this letter ASAP, June. We can't afford any more delays.'

'I was wondering if you could post it, Robert? Rachel and I have a lot to do this morning.'

I pretended not to hear her and got up to leave.

'Right, I am off to No. 10, key seats meeting.' June looked sceptical. Rachel said a beaming good luck.

'Don't forget our research project, Rachel. Looking forward to working with you on that.' Rachel beamed again.

I had nothing in my diary that morning, so sat in the Portcullis House café, hoping someone important would notice me. Three coffees filled an hour. I grew restless and dropped in on a meeting of the All-Party Parliamentary Group on poultry farming. Two guests, a florid-faced member of the National Farmers Union and a man in a pink shirt from one of the big animal charities, were having an argument about beak trimming, while MPs doodled. I asked both whether there was any link between beak trimming and salmonella rates, didn't listen to the answers and used my phone to draft a press release: 'Holton MP leads Parliamentary discussions on the Great British Egg'. The argument between the two guests escalated, until the NFU man – his face now brick red and the buttons on his straining check shirt popping open – accused his opponent of wanting to starve farmers to death. Pink shirt threw up his hands and left the room. The APPG Chair, an elderly Lib Dem Peer, decided that this resolved the matter and drew the meeting to a close.

As we were shuffling out, Mary Miles grasped my arm.

Mary was an esteemed barrister and a veteran government whip, tasked with keeping an eye on the new intake – including me. By dint of being basically invisible, I had so far avoided a bollocking. A gimlet sparkle in her eye suggested that this era may be coming to an end.

'How you are doing, Robert?'

Before I had a chance to answer, she continued, in the tight, menacing tones of the prosecuting counsel.

'I heard that you were seen heading to the Red Lion at quite an early hour yesterday. 3.11 pm to be precise. I hope Parliament isn't proving too much for you. If you are feeling overwhelmed, tired even, we can arrange' – a long pause – 'relief.'

I blustered something about meeting a local party donor, who had an interest in pubs. She raised an eyebrow. 'Don't grow breaking down on us, Robert. We need your skills on the green benches. Whatever they may prove to be.' She broke off to hold a door open for the elderly Lib Dem, and there the lesson endeth.

Yesterday surfaced again, with sharp contours. I had to confront this. I had to make sure I wasn't breaking down. Research time.

The House of Commons Library is everything you would imagine it to be. Dark panelling, deep wallpaper, great thick curtains of Victorian velvet keeping the modern world out. Leatherbound Hansards decay sedately, the words of long dead MPs trickling as dust into the open mouths of snoozing successors. Even the division bell is hushed, a gentle sigh of summons rather than the shill alarm of elsewhere in the Palace. The attendants wear slippers, and some of the MPs nightcaps.

I started with a 1930s history of Parliament, full of references to the 'Seat of Empire'. The book gushed through the history of Westminster, from a malaria-ridden Saxon monastery in a marsh, to a second-rate medieval palace, through to the port-addled squires that somehow fumbled modern Parliamentary democracy into being. I flicked all the way through the great fire that burned the place down in 1834, and the Victorian rebuilding that followed, without mention of anything remotely supernatural. The index confirmed it – galoshes, yes; gibbons, yes; gunpowder, yes – ghosts, no. Searches for spirits, visions, manifestations and phantoms also failed.

I turned to more informal sources. The diaries of former members, published to bore posterity, take up a full aisle of the library. Separated by many years, the diaries are all basically the same. The MP bitches about every colleague they have, deplores that their status does not match their perceived worth and drops delicate hints about their sexual preferences.

I skimmed through a representative sample. Horatio Fitzwilliam-Pinnington spent more than 40 pages explaining how an unholy combination of Fenians and Methodists were keeping him from the Colonial Office on the basis of moustache envy and dedicated precisely one sentence on his wife (she was to follow him on to a country weekend, along with 'the rest of heavy baggage'). Freddy 'fingers' Darlington described Lloyd George as an 'ungrateful Welsh tramp' and moaned about how tiresome all the war stuff was getting. Felix Egerton mixed sorrowful musings on the adverse consequences of having once coughed on Ted Heath at a cocktail party with a 400-stanza poem about an Irish Guardsman, St James Park and the 'naughtiest hour of night'. Aside from their self-regard, none of them strayed beyond the bounds of this world.

I kept looking. Histories, biographies, even a guide to Parliament written for new MPs in the Blair era (jolly font, glossy photos, shoulder pads). Still nothing.

Despairing after a few hours, I went over to the librarian's desk. He was a little, mole-like man, in the dusty black uniform of servants of the Commons, busy poring over some papers.

'Sorry to disturb you, I am struggling to find…'

He shot back, without looking up. 'If you are after some stats, one of my colleagues in the research department should be able to help you. This is not a place for numbers.'

'No, my question is a historical one.'

He looked up for the first time. 'Ah, well there I may be able to help. What is your area of interest?'

'Ghosts, on the Parliamentary estate. There don't seem to be any, and I wondered why.'

His deep brown eyes twinkled and seemed to become darker – almost black. He got up and looked around the library. Apart from him and I, there was one elderly peer in a far corner, fast asleep.

'Come with me, sir. We don't want to disturb anybody.'

He led me to a small door, set so closely with the panelling of the library as to be almost indistinguishable from it. It opened to a small, whitewashed corridor, festooned with electrical wires. We walked down until we reached another door. A wooden notice on it said, 'Ice Room'. The door opened to windowless space, featuring a small kitchen unit, a stack of chairs and a pile of ancient typewriters. The room smelt of old tea and wet sugar.

A lot of Parliament is like this. The Palace was built by the Victorians as a mini-London within London, with everything the discerning MP would need contained within its walls. Flower shops, bars (of course), hairdressers, even a shooting range. This was the capital's finest gentleman's club, and no gentleman need step outside its sacred walls for any pleasure. As the sunlit pomp of the 19th century faded during the long drizzle of the 20th, and the public purse shrank with the bounds of empire, these facilities became harder to justify. Service after service stopped, and space after space after space became redundant. Goodbye dedicated room for the storage of gin-and-tonic ice, hello junk cupboard.

I was feeling rather chuffed to have seen one of Parliament's lost rooms. Knowing their location helps mark you out as a proper Parliamentarian, and impresses visiting constituents. I had started to ask the librarian more about the room when he cut across me.

'Would you know a ghost if you saw one?'

I was a bit taken aback and didn't say anything.

'Think about it, sir. Parliament is a very busy place, with hundreds of strangers coming and going every day. Would you know if one them was' – he gave a thin smile – 'not of the land of the living?'

'I suppose not.'

'That lady in the old-fashioned dress, sitting on a bench. That man in the coat, hurrying down the corridor. The policeman with the strange helmet. All ghosts, about their business. Why, a lot of us house servants wear uniforms that haven't changed in hundreds of years. I could be a ghost.'

His eyes twinkled black again. I felt the hairs go up on the back of my neck.

'You asked, sir, why there are no ghosts in Parliament. There are, but most don't see them.'

'What about' – I gulped my rising fear down – 'those who do, um, see something?'

'You know this place, sir. Lots of people trying to be impressive, be the big serious politician. No one wants to sound silly. Can you imagine how much your colleagues would laugh if you told them you had seen a ghost? And think of the opposition. And the papers. MPs see ghosts. Some even recognise them for what they are. They just never, ever talk about it.'

The lack of any ghostly mentions in the diaries made sense suddenly. A fumble with a stranger in a public toilet was character, a glimpse of exciting human flaws, to make the grave statesmanship of the rest of life all the more impressive. Seeing dead people was a weakness of the head. Gladstone was a great man, who had a penchant for masturbating over sex workers. He didn't see elves dancing in the woods.

I took another big gulp. 'Do you know, umm, if there have been any ghosts seen with a moustache? An old gentleman, I mean. With a waistcoat. And maybe a pipe. Turns up, then disappears. Umn, anything like that reported?'

Another queer sparkle crossed the librarian's eyes. 'I don't know about that. Sounds like private business, sir.'

The final word hung in the musty space. The air felt charged. Time to go.

I made up a pathetic excuse about having a meeting to go to and he showed me out, back down the corridor and through the panelled door, back to the real world. The sight of the sleeping peer and the muffled sounds of bustle from outside the library were unexpectedly comforting. The library clock showed the time as 5 pm – I had lost hours in the place.

I was making mumbled thanks to the librarian and preparing for a swift exit when another man appeared suddenly beside us.

The librarian cleared his throat. 'Ah yes – a messenger for you, sir.' I felt suddenly very uncomfortable again. I wondered how he knew the messenger was for me, as no one had spoken.

The newcomer was wearing a palace uniform I hadn't seen before – black stockings, a dark green coat and silver buttons all along it. Come to think of it, I hadn't heard the title messenger before either.

The man's face was pitted, as with the scars of some dreadful skin disease. His eyes were silver grey, and when he spoke it was with an accent that sounded a little of the West Country, but with a curious lilt. 'A constituent is waiting for you, sirrah. In the lobby of St Stephen's. He wishes to discourse with you.'

'Discourse?' Fucking freak. And fucking cheeky constituent – coming into the Palace without an appointment. I flirted with the idea of ignoring the summons and making the wanker's journey futile, but felt the librarian's hand on my back, steering me out of the door. 'You really better go. Thank you for popping by the library.'

I followed the freak down through corridors, down staircases, through central lobby (making sure to get in the shot of a news camera, taking purposeful and important strides) and into St Stephen's Chapel. St Stephen's is built on the exact site, and to the same dimensions, as the old chapel Parliament met in from the reign of King Henry VIII to the great fire of 1834. The Victorians rebuilt it, in classic Victorian bad taste, as a shrine to English democracy, replete with hideous statues of Parliamentarians long dead and garish wall paintings, showing fever-dream versions of various key points in English history. Fittingly for our democracy, it also marks the furthest point members of the public can penetrate Westminster – they are welcome to linger in the past but are refused access to the reality of power behind the heavy oak doors at one end. Cocky constituents occasionally turn up to exercise their right to sit in the space and ask their MPs to come to meet them, a sure way of making sure that their representative will hate them, and whatever bullshit cause they are promoting, forever.

The freak lifted his arm to point out my constituent, visible only as a pair of knees behind one of the statues. A wisp of smoke was drifting up from the vicinity. 'He can't smoke in here, can he?' The freak gave a small, cold smile. 'Rules changes according to the times, so I have heard tell.' Fucking weirdo. I strode over to behind the statue, looking forward to administering a telling off.

'Hello boy.'

It was him, of course. Black three-piece suit, a fob watch across the waistcoat, thick neck and face, adorned with a white walrus moustache and a puffing brown pipe.

Two emotions flared in me: freezing fear, and a desire to confront, to understand. The latter won in a few seconds (somewhat to my surprise). I screwed my courage into a tight ball and spat it out through my mouth.

'You were in the Red Lion. What do you want? What do you want with me?'

His voice was public-school English, deeper and more real than mine.

'To work with you. On a matter of mutual advantage. You'll meet again won't you.'

It was a command, not a question. I nodded.

'Capital. I'll let you know. It will be in the constituency.'

'The constituency?'

'Yours and mine. Watch out for my message, and until then – stay out of trouble. My boy.' He winked, like some ghastly parody of an uncle, and then vanished. Again.

I turned, to check the freak had seem him too. The freak was nowhere.

It was an American tourist who revived me from my faint, pouring lukewarm Diet Coke into my mouth and wafting her cheap perfume up my nose. A little circle of the anxious and the rubbernecking had formed around where I had fallen, and the chapel was full of excited chatter. Things felt real and solid again. After thanking my rescuer with an autograph and a selfie, I went back to the library.

I wasn't really that surprised when, despite repeated

enquiries, no trace of a mole-like librarian, or pock-marked messenger, could be found. What turned out to be the only member of library staff, a young man with braided hair and tattoos all up his arms, did find out for me that the last messenger to be employed by the House of Commons had died in 1934. There was no door in the panelling of the wall.

Chapter 4

The rest of the week passed by in a blur of solitary gin, solitary coke and solitary insomnia, until I found myself deep in Friday.

Fridays are non-sitting days in Parliament. MPs head back to their constituencies, swapping the elite of Westminster for the meek of the earth. If they were only bloody meek. Constituency days mean being grumbled, shouted and occasionally spat at by people who see you as the personification of everything they hate, everything they have failed to do, and everything that will be done to them. A gauntlet of hate, to get you in the mood for the weekend.

This constituency day was starting with a meeting with a proper, bona fide bastard. Alfie Dalton was the terror of the village of Morton Babcock, a cider famer with 300 acres, 4 Rottweilers and zero tolerance of what he called 'cheek'. As his definition of cheek stretched from women wearing make-up, through to the existence of the minimum wage, he was a hard man to love.

He was also a Conservative Party donor, so love him I did. That morning I was sitting uncomfortably close to Alfie, in a decrepit old jeep that had last had road tax paid on it when Harold Wilson was Prime Minister. The rust bucket, festooned with faded Countryside Alliance stickers, jolted up and down as Alfie drove me, and my constituency caseworker Adam, through orchards smelling heavily of pesticide, with ill-looking sheep munching the yellow grass underneath the trees. One of the sheep looked very ill indeed, huge but strung out like a runner bean.

'It's an alpaca.' Alfie's voice, like his breath, was thick with last night's whiskey. 'The leggy brutes kill foxes. Stamp 'em underneath their hooves, mashing them to jam. Bet you did know that, eh?'

I made a polite mumble and tried not to think about vomit. My body felt strange after four days of intoxicants and worry, eyes like poached eggs, brain like cotton wool in a rainstorm.

The jeep gave a particularly savage lurch, leaning at a 45-degree angle to the ground for a few moments, before righting itself. As we drew level again, Alfie muttered 'fuck pit' cryptically. Ten seconds of silence, then 'you gits are doing all right on the brocks'. I racked my weary brain for a clue as to what he was on about and drew a blank. I glanced back at Adam and he mouthed 'todger' at me. I furrowed my brow. He mouthed again. 'Tadger'? He drew his finger across his throat.

'Badger cull! You mean the badger cull, Alfie?'

'Of course I do you dozy fuck. Brocks are badgers. Course you come from the city, bloody

nonce.'

I decided to ignore the abuse and accept the praise. 'I am glad the policy is working for you, Alfie. It's been tough, but we made the adult, necessary decision to allow the shooting of badgers to stop the spread of the dreadful bovine TB. Farmers are the backbone of this great…'

Alfie cut me off with a colossal clearing of his throat, and the ejection of a grenade of sputum past my face and out of my window. 'I don't shot the fuckers. I gas 'em. Trap 'em, gas 'em, chuck 'em in the pit.'

Conversation languished after that.

After a few more minutes of horrid jolting, we came to a ramshackle barn, nestled in a dank hollow of land. A very dead sheep was rotting outside. 'Been meaning to take that to the fuck pit.' I wished he would stop saying fuck pit. He opened the door of the barn and we stepped through into a space that stank of mildew and sweat. A couple of dirty mattresses were pushed against one wall, a Portaloo teetered against another. A sheep dip took up one corner, with a bottle of Radox shower gel perched on it.

'This where the polaks live – looks aright, don't it?'

We had reached the greasy nub of our visit. Alfie was under investigation by the Farming Standards Agency following a complaint about how he treated his farm workers – all from Eastern Europe. He had called on the mobile I keep reserved for Party donors and had asked, with his savage lyricism, for me to 'make this nonsense go away, so some more readies can come your way'. The constituency office needed a new printer.

'How many, em, workers live here typically, Alfie?'

'Maybe ten. Thereabouts. They come and go.'

Alife broke off to yell at Adam for taking notes. 'Don't do none of your recording, boy. I know your tricks.' Adam put the notebook away and became very interested in the barn roof.

'Fucking mini nonce. Anyway, where was I – yes, polaks. Come and go. They do theirs work, they get their readies, they fuck off. No complaints. No paperwork either.'

A belching laugh.

'They like it out here. Healthy, sort of outdoor life. Bit like back home for them – basically savages out there. They work hard though, will give 'em that. Not like you spoiled gits. Hands like girls.'

Adam folded his behind his back.

The smell from the Portaloo was making me nauseous. I had to get out, and quickly.

'I think we can sort this, Alfie. Tell you what – why don't you get a testimonial from one of your lads? I can write to the Chair of the Food Standards Agency. I met him at a reception a few months back, he will remember me. We'll sort it out no problem.'

Alfie grunted.

'Don't worry, Alfie, Adam will take charge and will work his usual magic. Won't you, Adam?'

Adam murmured.

'Adam, why don't you give Alfie your mobile number, then he has a direct line to you? For updates and such like.'

Adam shot me a remember-my-girlfriend-is-a-journalist glare. I dropped the idea.

'Yes, Alfie, find one of your chaps who likes it here, get him to write down how much fun he is having, and I can send it on to the Agency Chair.'

Something scuttled in the Portaloo.

'Is one of the lads here? I would like to meet them.' (You never know when someone might gain settled status, and with that voting rights.)

'Nah, you dozy prick – they're working. What do you think I pay 'em for? What do you think I pay you for?'

Another horrid laugh, followed by horrid phlegm.

He scratched one of the redder bits of his red nose. 'That'll be a rat. They like to swim in the bowl, crafty buggers.'

Alfie drove us back to the farm where the car was parked, spitting the whole way. He made us drink some scrumpy that tasted like horse hair and burnt dung ('my finest fruits for you fine fruits') then waved us off the property, shotgun under one arm.

We went back to the office, via an early lunch in the Hare and Garter. When I started this job, I have grand visions of Adam and I discussing the day's work over a pint, me wise and kind, him spaniel loyal and respectfully adoring. In reality, Adam refuses to drink before 6 and raises an eyebrow whenever I do. He has a J20 and we make stilted conversation about weekend plans, and both check our phones. Occasionally he asks me when he can move to work in Parliament (every constituency staffer's one dream is this) and casually mentions that his journalist girlfriend has an open offer from a London paper and would love to move too. I blame June and buy him a pudding.

Truth is, Adam is too good at his job to move him. Every MP needs an Adam – someone to keep the constituency ticking over, do a share of the face-to-face meetings and generally keep the flag flying. Someone competent enough to inspire some confidence with the local bigwigs, but too young looking to be seen as any sort of rival. He also kept the office in good nick – as we arrived after lunch it smelt of beeswax polish and hoovering. He presented me with a neatly stacked and well-ordered set of papers, and made me coffee darker and stronger than sin. I told him that, if politics fell through, he would make an excellent butler. He said that he was happy to be Jeeves to my Bertie Wooster. We both pretended to laugh.

Halfway through my papers, Rachel called. She rattled through a few Parliamentary invites (yes to those with booze, no to those without), asked how the weather was in Holton and then, almost an afterthought, said, 'Oh, and the ghost project, I turned up something interesting.'

The cold feeling that I had kept at bay with booze, coke and pretending to work came back.

'Are you still there, sir?'

Even the 'sir' didn't bring back any warmth. 'Yes, carry on.'

'Well, I looked online for stuff about MPs and ghosts,

just like you said. There wasn't much – but there was a blog from, well, you'll never guess.'

I croaked try me.

'Dr Duncan Middleton, your predecessor. You know when he went a bit funny when they bailed out the banks?'

Duncan's shredding sense of the purpose of a Labour government, and with that himself, had reached a low point in 2008. He took three weeks off to walk the path of the Jarrow march, had shaved off his hair and started writing daily blogs, featuring his own poetry.

'Well, around that time – in a blog piece called the long, winding and red road – he mentioned that he had been visited by a dead man. Someone who had been an MP for Holton in the past apparently.'

I forced firmness into my voice. 'How interesting. What happened?'

'The man, well, ghost I suppose, poured Dr Middleton a whiskey and told him to buck up. The he vanished. Dr Middleton said it had been rather comforting. Actually, that was the last blog he wrote before he checked into that clinic.'

I thanked Rachel for the information, wished her a good weekend, hung up and went to the loo. After mopping up brow sweat and liberally applying cold water, I examined my eyeballs. Definitely a bit yellow around the edges. I stayed locked in the toilet for 15 minutes, until Adam knocked on the door, asked (with some relish) if the lunchtime prawns had been dodgy and told me it was time for my advice surgery.

It was the usual advice surgery fare. A man with wild hair wanting help with overturning an RSPCA investigation into cruelty against goats, a large woman smelling of cheese who wanted her neighbour evicted for having 'gentlemen over after hours', and an elderly pervert trying to get a visa for a much younger wife from Thailand. I was distracted for the duration, but just about held it together. My sympathetic face has been carefully carved over the years and, combined with a few nods and affirmative noises, it usually suffices. After the surgery, Adam works out what to do, and how best to gently let down the no hopers.

The last appointment that day fell firmly into the no-hoper category. Tommy Dallinger was a little crab apple of a person, with deep brown eyes. Tattoos swirled up both of his arms, circular patterns that came together at the top of his chest, to form the face of a bearded man, with antlers growing from his head. At the edge of the beard, leaves swirled, and dived down, until they were lost to sight beneath a grubby v-neck.

Tommy saw me looking. 'It's Herne the Hunter. Well, some call him the green man, but I call him Herne. He is a spirit you know, a huntsman of old. He still guards Windsor Forest. I grew up there. It's my soul home, an old wood, with an old spirit protecting it.'

I wanted to ask him more, but Adam interjected, suggesting that time was short and that Tommy better get on with his story.

It was, as surgery tales go, an interesting one. As implied by the full-body tattoo, Tommy had drained the 1960s dry. Starting the decade as a garage mechanic, he had finished it as a druid, travelling around the festival circuit in a polka-dot caravan, 'soaking in the wisdom, letting out the joy'. He had lived off a comprehensive knowledge of where to find magic mushrooms, like some psychedelic cabbie, and a retained ability to keep the tattered vehicles of the flower children on the road. He had chanted, vomited and fornicated his way from Essex mudflats to Somerset meadows, from mountain woods in the Pennines to star-hung Cornish beaches. He had survived a blow from a policeman's truncheon at Stonehenge in the 80s, an adverse reaction to new pills in the 90s, and a mounting sense that the party was ending in the 2000s. A few years ago he had bowed to the inevitable, hanging up robes, selling his van to a collector and enquiring about how he could collect his pension.

The answer was that he had no pension worth the name to collect. Tommy had checked out of society in the golden summer of 1964, when things were getting better and better, and kind old Mr Wilson was busy seeing everyone right. He had checked back in in colder, harder times. At a DWP office in Swindon, isolated like a plague victim behind Perspex glass, he had been informed that 40 years of wisdom gleaned from the astral realm was not the same thing as having 40 years of National Insurance contributions. He was due £321.27 from the state, for his distant mechanic days. The sum had been given to him that afternoon, counted to the last penny. He was then discharged, from the care of the state into that of the street.

Since then, he had wandered the Southwest, living off odd jobs, ignoring the growing agony in his hips, kipping on sofas, and trying to prove that the pension he had long counted on was still owed to him. He had his 'papers', a collection of receipts and scraps of memories committed to paper, rustling in a pink plastic bag, which he put on the office table.

'Look through my papers, it's all there. You can sort it out, show that I was working. Please. I am here for another three weeks, before I have to clear out of my current place.'

I watched Adam take a despairing look at the bag, and the yellowing, disordered papers seeping out of it. A gleam of inspiration suddenly struck him.

'Mr Dallinger, are you a permanent resident in this constituency?'

With the simplicity of an earlier age, Tommy said he was

not, he had just been offered some floor space here for a month. With sorrowful firmness, Adam explained that we could only assist people with a permanent address in the constituency.

Tommy was, at least, now used to official disappointment and trooped out quietly, taking his bag with him.

'Adam, I feel a bit bad about this one. Isn't there anything more we can do?'

'People like that, they are their own worst enemies. Chaotic, always will be. He would just spend the pension on drugs anyway. Look, if you really want, I'll go and give him a food bank referral. It is a waste, but I can do it.'

'Yes, thank you. I really appreciate you going the extra mile with this one.'

With a sigh, Adam headed out into the hallway after Tommy. My duty done, I put the matter from my mind, put my feet up on the table and searched my own name on Twitter.

Adam came back after a minute or two, looking a little put out.

'You have a letter – must have been hand delivered just now. I don't understand why people can't just use the post.'

'Probably because we privatised Royal Mail.'

My self-affirming laugh died in my throat as I saw the letter. The envelope was rich, creamy paper, sealed in wax – the inscription written in flowing ink 'Mr Robert Wilkes, Member of Parliament for Holton and the District'. It was also covered in a thick layer of dust.

Words from St Stephen's came back to me, in all their grim certainty: 'Watch for my message'.

I opened it slowly. The letter was typewritten, and had a faded portcullis in one corner.

'Dear boy,

The time has come to meet and have a proper discussion, man to man. Meet me at Wilmington Butts at 9 pm tonight. Come alone and on foot.

It will be to your advantage.
Yours sincerely,
Maurice Copeland-Ellis'

I grimaced through the final meeting of the day (local National Farmers Union reps, grumbling about being prevented from using a new, exciting and fatal-in-large-doses pesticide), sent Adam off home early and locked the door. Wikipedia confirmed all my horrible thoughts.

'Maurice Copeland-Ellis, born 12 January 1890, inherited Thorpe House in the Holton District of Gloucestershire from his father in 1911. Served as a Major with the Royal Gloucestershire Hussars in Palestine in WW1, elected as Conservative MP for Holton (a position his grandfather and great grandfather had each held) in 1924. Served as a backbencher for forty years, being described by Commons diarist Felix Egerton as 'the very embodiment of a Knight of the Shire'. Retired at the 1964 General Election and died in 1967.'

I wrote down the last three words in a notepad, stared at them, then repeated the exercise. It brought no ease.

Deciding this was all a hoax also provided scant comfort. Every time I convinced myself that I was the victim of a cruel trick, maybe conducted by June, I remembered the disappearing act. June could vanish hope, mirth, joy – but not people.

I was left with two outcomes. Either I was mad, or a ghost wanted to meet me. My mind shuddered between the two for an hour, until it felt bruised from the bouncing. I had to know. I decided to go to Wilmington Butts early.

It was an early May evening, and the sun was shining. An air of drowsy contentment filled the lanes as I drove out of Holton and deep into old Gloucestershire. Wilmington Butts is an iron-age hillfort by the River Yaddle, nothing more than a few low banks of earth now, overgrown with gorse. It was used as a gathering point for centuries; evangelical preachers and politicians used to give open-air addresses there well until the 20th century. Only sheep and the odd archaeologically minded tourist visit it now. I had been only once, to have some pre-election photos taken (tie with pheasants on it, sleeves rolled up, manly stubble), and had to ask directions twice.

Eventually I spotted a footpath sign at the corner of the road, with 'Wilmington Butts, 1.5 miles' inscribed on it. Underneath, another sign: 'Access by foot only'. Fuck the countryside.

I parked up snug on a verge, had one last swig from the whiskey bottle that lives in the glove compartment, and started walking. The footpath ran through a large field, where the green spring corn was yellowing after the first few days of hot sunshine. Poppies were sprouting amid the stalks, swallows were swooping and the gentle buzz of insects rang from the hedges. I felt oddly calm and, realising that it was only just past seven, decided to wait a bit. I sat under an oak tree, took my shoes and socks off and let my bare feet radiate in the warmth coming up from the ground. I fell into a whiskey doze, and then – unexpectedly – into sleep.

When I awoke, darkness was falling. The field felt less peaceful now. The hedge rustled. The oak above me creaked, almost as if it was tensing. It was like the place was waiting for something.

My phone said it was ten minutes to nine. I hurried along the path by the hedge's edge, using the phone as a torch.

There was a gentle woosh to my left, and in the last of the light I saw a heron lazily gliding along the hedge line. It was moving very slowly, and never left my eyeline. After a couple of minutes I hit the River Yaddle. The hedges and fields fell away, and I walked on with the river to one side and wet pasture to my other. The heron still pressed on ahead of me.

I noticed some trees to one side of the path but couldn't bring myself to look at that concentrated darkness. There, the night was a being, not hostile as such, but not benevolent either – an alien presence, watching and waiting.

My inner calm was fading fast. I went to check my emails, to remind myself of the real, workaday world – of deadlines, Ccs and kind regards – but my phone went dead in my hand. I had borrowed Adam's charger in the office and it must have been a dud. Must have been. A cold mist was rising from the river, and before long I could no longer see my feet, then my knees, then my thighs. Only the glint of the river stretching out in front of me, and the heron soaring noiselessly above it, guided me on.

I started to become aware of other things flapping near me, darting down into the mist, flitting across the water and then soaring upwards. Bats. I flirted with running back down the path, towards my car. It was only the thought that this would mean that whatever was waiting for me at the Butts would then be behind that stopped me. I reminded myself that I was Robert Wilkes, elected Member of Parliament, a man elected and sometimes respected by his peers. I walked on.

There was a splash, and I felt water seeping into my shoes. I had walked straight into the river. I swore at the mist and hit out at it. It broke before my hand to reveal water all around my feet. A reflected moon glittered on the surface of the river. I looked up to see the original glowing yellow in the black sky. Something bristled against the sodden hem of my trousers I glanced back down. Scores of dark fish, with bulbous eyes and dark green scales, were brushing against my legs. They swam in a circle, going faster and faster. Above, bats echoed their dance, swirling around me. Nature was in a frenzy, and I was in the centre of it.

I stumbled out of the river, closing my eyes as I felt the leather of bats' wings on my cheek. I regained the path, and with it the heron, who was now walking ahead of me, with great, slow, deliberate strides, like some cadaverous clergyman approaching an altar, mist trailing behind him.

An earthen bank rose up in front of us, with a gap in the middle, which the path ran straight through. Beyond the gap it was pitch black; even the fog didn't seem to want to enter. The heron entered.

Channelling the last of my courage into four steps, I followed it in.

Darkness, silence, cold.

And then a flash, a burst, an atomic blast of light, white light, suffusing everything. After a few seconds, the white light narrowed and flickered, to a yellow flame just ahead of me.

'Welcome to Wilmington Butts. A historic, ancient place. Nearly as ancient as me.'

And there the bastard was. Sitting on a mound, an old paraffin lamp beside him. He was in a tweed suit this time, with a tweed hat of the kind that only fly fishermen and young Conservatives wear. His eyes were just the same as before, piercing blue. They twinkled obscenely in the yellow light of the lamp.

I felt a sudden, unexpected surge of anger that burnt away my fear. The coldness in my bones gave way to the rising heat of rage. Every ordinary, sensible part of me rose up in rebellion at this apparition, this absurdity. This was ridiculous. There was a ghost waiting for me. A fucking ghost.

'You know what, you can fuck off. Fuck right off. Fucking cunt. I have had enough of this. Fuck off back to fairyland.'

He simply smiled. 'Very unparliamentary language.'

'You know, I don't believe in you.' Somewhere in my brain, I was hoping that these words would have a decisive effect, making him vanish like some vast, hairy Tinkerbell.

He remained very much present.

'I get it, I am having a breakdown. I am seeing things. Seeing you. I am going to go to a therapist, get some pills and you are going to disappear.'

There was no reaction. 'You will be gone. Kapow.'

I mimed empty air. 'You are nothing. You don't exist.'

He took a deep suck at his pipe and blew. Hot, spiced smoke filled my nose and mouth. I started choking.

'Seems pretty real to me, boy.' Another curl of smoke enveloped me, like mustard gas with added pepper.

I struggled for breath, tears starting from my eyes. I gasped for cleaner air.

'Very well, enough.' He knocked his pipe out on the earth. 'Now I have presented my credentials, perhaps we can have a chat. I assume – being the clever boy you are – that you have looked me up in a library by now?'

I coughed the last of the smoke out of my lungs. 'You're Maurice. Used to be MP for here. Died in…'

'Yes, died in January 1967. Mouth cancer. All very unpleasant. Still, over it now though.'

He laughed, a great belly chuckle, and looked at me to join in.

'How are you here? Why are you here?'

'You mean here precisely? This is old land, with thousands of years of stories flowing through it. The more stories, the easier it is to slip back in, past the veil. I am a water droplet of story, and this place is a river of stories. Means I can stay this side longer. Have a proper conversation.'

'The veil? This side?'

'Look, we can talk theology if you wish. However, you don't strike me as someone too interested in how many angels fit on the head of a pin. I suspect you might be more interested in what I have come to talk to you about.'

'Have you come to talk to me about the milk of human kindness? About my misspent youth and selfish ways? Am I going to wake up, on Christmas Day, and have to buy a huge fucking turkey?'

'I want to talk to you about your career.'

'Is this a mentoring session?'

'Of a sort. I was the Member of Parliament for Holton for many years. I looked after this place, this land, and the people who live on it. I would like to continue doing this, through you.'

'How exactly?'

'That hostile tone again, boy. We need to fix that. People won't warm to you. If you are to go far, we must polish you up. And you are to go far, I am resolved on that.'

Amid the anger and confusion broiling in the pit of my stomach, I felt a flower bloom. All predictions of future greatness are welcome, even from a dead man.

'Go on.'

'You should see me as a guide. Someone to steer you in the right direction. Point out the pitfalls, and the opportunities. With my help, you can climb that ladder. And the higher you climb – the better for Holton.'

'And for Netley and Pilford?'

A patrician wrinkle of the nose. 'Even for them.'

He put his pipe in his pocket. 'I am offering you the deal of a lifetime, boy. Expert guidance. An advisor who has seen it all. And who can slip through doors, without being seen. Think of me as a fly on the wall. A big, clever fly, working for you.'

'No one works for anyone, not for free. What's in it for you?

He smiled at me. 'You have a lot of talent, Robert. There is a reason I have chosen you – you have it. A great mind, a real connection to people. You can be the MP I never was. You can get there. No. 10.'

The magic words hung in the air.

'Yes, I can get you to the top. And from there you can do wonderful things for Holton. That's what is in it for me – to know that the place I loved is being looked after.'

I looked up, hoping the stars would tell me what the fuck to do. There were no stars, only the huge, yellow moon.

'Come on, boy, come with me to No. 10. Make an old man very happy.'

No. 10.

'Look, it's late, I am tired. This is all bonkers. Too bonkers to think about. Let's say I just accept all this, take it at face value.'

'Capital notion. Much less stressful all round.'

'Hmm, well if I do, what next? What do you need me to do?'

'For now, just to shake on our agreement. Like gentlemen.'

He held out his hand.

I felt sick, but forced myself to offer mine. I imagined a screaming nothingness meeting my fingers, or wet, rotting flesh, or somehow the worst – cold bone.

Instead, my fingers started to tingle with warmth, with the hairs on my arm standing to attention. As he enfolded my hand in his, darts like electricity shot through my arm.

'Excellent, we are agreed.'

He kept his hand on mine, and the bolts of electricity twinged up into my arm, and deep into my chest. The sensation was not unpleasant.

'I am so glad you took the sensible course. I will be in

touch with you very soon, watch out for my letter. Cheerio – and lay off the marching powder. No scandals for a future prime minister.'

He guffawed, and with his laugh the blinding light came again. I felt it in my chest, bursting out and filling the old hillfort like a great white breath.

The air crackled, and then there was darkness.

I came to curled up and alone, what must have been many hours later. A warm May dawn was breaking. Birds were singing and warm sunshine lapped around me like balm. I straightened up, brushed down my suit and walked to the top of the earthen bank. The river stretched beneath it, glittering joyfully in the morning light. A heron flapped lazily over the waters.

Chapter 5

I love giving tours of Parliament. Constituents visiting London make appointments to visit, fit in an hour between being fleeced at Madame Tussauds and getting mugged on the Southbank, and receive the full blast of my charm. The work is easy, the attention is flattering and opportunities to look impressive abound.

A week after Wilmington Butts I was in full genial guide mode, with a family from one of the more up-itself streets in Netley that were as gullible as they were large. Mr Noakes was a stalwart of the rugby club going rapidly to seed, Mrs Noakes sold life insurance to people who should know better, and the younger Noakes had the greasy pubescence that comes with excess eating and unsupervised internet use.

I had brought the family first to the Victoria Tower entrance, the least used but grandest bit of the Palace, and had tickled them like trout round the gilt-hung rooms. Mrs Noakes nearly wet herself with delight at the toilet, hidden by panelling, only used by the Queen on state visits. Mr Noakes said that huge, hideous paintings of Trafalgar and Waterloo 'make a chap proud to be British'. When I told him the out-and-out lie that the paintings had to be covered up whenever the President of France visited 'to save their blushes', he chortled, like a pig being fellated.

We passed through the Lords, and Mrs Noakes said that the vast golden throne would look good in their living room. I pointed out the glowering statues of the 16 barons who forced King John to sign the Magna Carta, to blank faces. Mr Noakes took an important phone call in central lobby about his new conservatory, while the younger Noakes tried to get in the shot of the BBC News at One camera. Mr Noakes finishing his call by shouting that he would sue if he didn't get a 20% discount and then took a photo of Mrs Noakes trying to look sexy underneath a statue of Gladstone.

I ushered them into the Commons, and away from the disapproving glare of the stewards. In my best blokey style, I whispered to Mr Noakes that a famous TV chef had been deflowered against the Speaker's Chair. He nudged me in the ribs, kept his elbow there a little too long, and Mrs Noakes said that she would have to keep an eye on naughty lads like us. I had sudden horrid visions of suburban threesomes – meaty kisses, meaty thighs, flavoured lube. I switched to cholera, painting a grimly vivid picture of the 'shithouse Parliament' of 1856, and the three days of hosing down that was required before the chamber could be used again. The Noakeses moved away.

The fatter of the younger Noakes tried to sit on one of the green benches. I took the opportunity to lift him up by the scruff of his neck, to prevent ample posterior meeting ample seat. I explained to him that if any unelected person sat on the benches, the law required them to be locked up in the Tower of London, on a diet of bread and water. The last part of the threat seemed to hit home, and he fell into sulky acquiescence. I rattled through the remaining hoary anecdotes – seats placed a sword's length apart to prevent duelling, each chair has a potty underneath it, a pair of Queen Victoria's knickers

in each dispatch box – and had them nodding apprecia-
tively along to each lie.

We headed into one of the voting lobbies beside the col-
umns, and I explained in great detail how – although anti-
quated – the venerable British tradition of counting each
voting MP in a great line was far more reliable than the
glitzy but fundamentally unreliable online voting systems
abroad. Mr Noakes was made very happy by this com-
parison. I tipped him over to ecstasy by pointing out a
hollow on a windowsill (created by weevils) and stating
confidently that Churchill had used it as an ashtray for
his cigars while waiting to vote. Mr Noakes was positively
purring by now, and I was confident that he would be
sending a glowing report back to his rugby club. 'A fine
chap, that Mr Wilkes. Sound man. Credit to the town.'
Lots of voters and donors at the club. Men with big stomachs and big wallets. Perhaps they would make me chair?
Little 'sparrow-legs Robbie', the toast of the rugby lads.
That would show those fuckers.

My daydreams were shattered by the sharp smell of sour
whiskey and over-applied cologne. Harry Crowther lurched
up before me, in a striped pink and green blazer and a yellow
shirt that had once been white. I tried to give him the brush
off – I wanted the Noakeses to see me on nodding terms
with Cabinet ministers, not with washed-up old drunks.
Too late, Harry was busy shaking Mr Noakes' hand and
patting the wet heads of the younger Noakeses. I could see
from the look in her eyes that Mrs Noakes already had him
marked down as an undesirable.

'Harry, what can I do for you? Mr and Mrs Noakes, Harry
is a veteran Member of Parliament, a real Westminster
original.'

'More like a Werther's Original, dear boy. Good for
sucking.'

'Not much time, Harry! Lots to see and that. How can I help?'

Harry was too drunk to register the impatience in my tone. 'I have a letter for you, old boy. From a real old boy.'

Maurice. The old fear from before lingered, overlain with a new excitement. This would be a good thing. A good, positive thing.

My hand trembled slightly as I took the letter from Harry's mottled fingers. It couldn't wait, I ripped the envelope open, trying to hide the contents from view. The letter was on the same yellowing paper as before, with the faded portcullis on the top.

My dear Robert,

It was very good to chat last week – I am delighted by our 'Wilmington Accord'.

As the first fruit of our agreement, I can pass on a rather interesting bit of information I heard while gliding between walls and scaring nurses in Gloucester. The Gloucester Hospital Chief Executive held a rather grand dinner last month for his local MP – and a rather distinguished guest. The dinner was paid for by the state.

I suggest you investigate further. Happy hunting.
Yours fraternally,
Maurice

'Mr and Mrs Noakes, please accept my apologies. This is a very important message from No. 10. I must leave at once.'

Harry looked confused. 'I don't think it came from there. It came from an old chap, one of the really old guard. I do see them you know, after a few drinks.'

I made a mental note to have a conversation with Harry at some point. Now, however, was the time for action.

'You and your nicknames for the Cabinet, Harry. Mr and Mrs Noakes, let me call my researcher Rachel. She can complete your tour for you. I am really sorry to have to leave you like this, but when No. 10 calls…'

The Noakeses looked suitably impressed. Before I could call Rachel, Harry offered to lead the rest of their tour, being 'at something of a loose end'.

Before I could intervene, Mr Noakes accepted the offer. I was too excited to argue and, after some hasty handshakes and an offer to speak at the next rugby club dinner, I sprinted off to my office. (I later learnt that, after a tour diversion to Strangers Bar, Mr Noakes and Harry packed the remaining Noakeses onto the Bristol train and spent the evening, next morning and afternoon drinking whiskey in Harry's flat. Mr Noakes left Netley, and his wife, very shortly after that. I never got my rugby club invite.)

Rachel and June were both in the office, the latter eating a boiled egg from a small Tupperware box.

'Can you open a window, June? Quite whiffy in here.'

With a face like thunder, she obliged. I decided that taking her seat would be too much and sat in the armchair.

'Rachel, I need to make a Freedom of Information request. You can do those, can't you?'

An obliging smile. 'Yes, of course. What do you need to know, sir?'

'It's a request to Gloucestershire Hospitals NHS Foundation Trust. About entertainment budgets.'

'On it.' A few minutes of typing, Rachel's concentration face (eyebrows furrowed, no blinking, nose wrinkled) and then a cluck of satisfaction. 'Right, fire away.'

I love giving dictation. 'To ask how much the Trust has spent on catering for the executive team over the last 60 days and i) all functions covered by that budget and ii) the names of all guests at each such function.'

'They will struggle to wriggle out of that one, sir. Should it go in under your name?'

'Probably best actually if it goes in under your name. Less political, um, complications that way.'

June piped up from the egg corner. 'I would imagine you would be safe, Robert. They won't know who you are either.'

A frosty silence fell, broken only by the tip tap of Rachel's typing and then – after a minute or so – by the creak of the door.

Rachel smiled – 'Emily! What good timing. You can meet the boss.'

The newcomer was a girl with mousey blonde hair, a snub nose and very brown eyes. She spoke in a breathless rush, with the elongated syllables of private school. 'Hullo, Mr Wilkes, great to meet you. Thank you so, so much for this wunderful opportunity.'

I racked my brains for a clue as to who she was. Distant memories of a conversation over coffee with Rachel surfaced. Rachel had been wearing a white dress. Something about an old school friend? A sister? Work experience.

'Ah yes, nice to meet you, Emily. How long are you with us for?'

'As long as you want, Mr Wilkes.' Was that a twinkle deep in those brown depths?

June intervened, like a bucket of ice-cold cod-liver oil. 'Emily is interning with us for the next 12 weeks. She is on a gap year. Between university – and school.'

'Great stuff, well I hope you enjoy your time here, Emily. I should take you for a tour and tea on the terrace at some point.'

A pronounced cough from June.

'Rachel and I can take you for a tour.'

'That would be lovely, thank you, Mr Wilkes.'

'That FOI request has been done, sir, all submitted.'

There was a new note of sharpness in Rachel's voice. Was it jealousy?

I resolved to come into the office more often over the next three weeks.

'I say, June, haven't you got a lot of holiday to take? Now we have Emily with us for a bit, why don't you take it? Go on that Saga cruise.'

June did not go on holiday. Still, by popping in whenever I knew she had bunked off early, I managed to spend some pleasant hours in the office with Emily and Rachel during what turned out to be a glorious May.

We would open a bottle of cheap prosecco – bought from the tiny Westminster Tesco that pulls a fetid feeding of the 5,000 miracle every day, replenishing bored Minister and bored tourist alike with soggy sandwiches and warm Coke – and drink it from plastic cups, while smoking out of the window. I would tell the girls outrageous political gossip, half true, half made up, and we would listen to protestors – just out of sight – yelling outside the gates of No. 10. One afternoon, in a fit of daring, I led them up winding Victorian staircases to the roof of the building and elbowed open a fire door to reveal a stunning panorama of the Whitehall skyline, glistening in the sun. I still have a selfie we took that afternoon, our grins huge, our faces flush with booze, their hair and my blue tie rippling in the breeze. We all look very happy.

I learnt more about both Rachel and Emily on those golden afternoons. It transpired that Emily was a friend of Rachel's sister – they had all gone to school together at one of those stately homes turned middle-class factories that litter the Surrey countryside and the Good Schools Guide. Rachel, two years older, had always kept a sisterly eye out for the younger two, through hockey team selection, rugby club parties and A-levels – and now in the big bad world beyond. Emily was always gushingly grateful to Rachel for 'giving me the chance to see where things happen' and retained an unfailing enthusiasm for even the grimmest grunt work she had to complete, from licking envelopes, to making the tea, to fetching the prosecco.

One evening, it waxed late. We had gone through two bottles of warm fizz, and had just started on the third. The air smelt of fresh booze – the sweet, gentle scent before droplets and evenings go stale. Every hour, the big Victorian clock in the office would chime, 30 seconds after Big Ben (I told the girls that it hadn't kept the right time since being jarred by a Second World War bomb). Rachel had put Abbey Road on, and the familiar sound formed the riverbed to our burblings. We were talking about their childhoods, about the moments that had made us happy, the nights that had made us cry. Emily said she thought joy was most undiluted when you were young, and that it made her sad to think that would never come again. Rachel reminded her that she was 19. We laughed until our stomachs hurt. Emily asked if my parents had helped make me 'the man you are today'.

I told them about my father. His humble roots, his construction business built from the ground up, the Thatcher boom and the year he switched from donkey jackets to tweed. With the warmth of the prosecco coursing through me, I managed to make his nicknames for me (nancy, wilting billy, nonce-breath), his ten pints a day habit and his mistress in Taunton sound like the peccadillos of an original John Bull, rather than the hallmarks of a cast-iron tosser. I even managed to inject some emotion into my voice when I spoke of the inevitable, overwhelming heart attack. I framed the monthly payments to my widowed mother as the caring act of a loving son, instead of the price for having her out of my life.

It might have been the after-effects of the laughing fit,

but Emily's eyes looked wet. She asked me to show her on the constituency map where I had grown up. As I got up to do so, she stood behind me. I could feel her breath on my neck. As I pointed out the Netley street I had been born in, and then the much posher one I had grown up in, she traced the line with her own finger, before leaving it to rest against mine. It stayed there, just as Here Comes the Sun came through the speakers.

Here comes the sun, do, dun, do, do
Here comes the sun, and I say
It's all right
Little darling, it's been a long cold lonely winter
Little darling, it feels like years since it's been here
Here comes the sun, do, dun, do, do
Here comes the sun, and I say
It's all right

After 20 or so seconds, Rachel said something, and we both stepped back. The thing unspoken in the air slid away, with the last beats of the chorus.

Rachel was keen to go after, saying it was a school night and was 'really quite late already'. The music was turned off and the empty prosecco bottles bundled into a bin bag, so June wouldn't spot them in the morning. At Westminster Bridge, they headed underground as I walked back across the bridge to my flat, humming.

The FOI reply from the Gloucestershire Hospitals NHS Foundation Trust came back the next day and the week got even better.

In the terse, clipped terms of officialdom, the reply stated that £2,201.46 had been spent on catering for the executive team over the last 60 days. The entirety of the cost came from a 'stakeholder dinner', held at La Piccolo restaurant (private room), with Henry Middleton (Gloucestershire Hospitals Chief Executive), Jane Sharp (Gloucestershire Hospitals Director of Growth), Richard Houston (Gloucestershire Hospitals Head of Maternity Services), Sir Roger Mapehurst (MP for Gloucester) and Nicholas Gorringe (MP for Little Rowley and Parliamentary Under Secretary of State, Department of Health). Gotcha.

My email was composed within five happy minutes.

Dear Sir Roger,

First, I wanted to congratulate you on your campaign to save the Bapington bakery from closure. I have, like so many others across the country and I dare say the world, been inspired by your unstinting efforts to 'keep the bap in Bapington'.

I am also writing to do you the courtesy of letting you know in advance of my intention to raise a question in the House concerning your constituency. It has come to my attention that more than £2,000 of public money was recently spent by Gloucestershire Hospitals NHS Foundation Trust on an expensive dinner. I understand that maternity services were on the agenda, that seven bottles of Château Lafite were on the table, and that a junior health minister was in the room.

I intend to raise this at the next Health Questions, to ask if the Secretary of State is prepared to explain why his Minister was in attendance and what the purpose of this splashing of taxpayer cash was.

I appreciate that the Minister in question being your son-in-law may make this issue a sensitive one for you. However, I know that you share my commitment to following through on our manifesto promises to cut waste in our health service, and to reduce the influence of backroom lobbying on public-sector decision making. I believe that the Secretary of State, and the public, will be keen to know all the details – sunlight really is the best disinfectant, isn't it?

Please don't hesitate to let me know if you would like to chat through further.
With all best wishes,
Rob
P.S Up the baps!

Negotiations were completed in one hour and sealed in whiskey at Sir Roger's club. At Health Questions, I watched as Sir Roger rose ponderously from his seat.

'Will my right honourable friend agree with me that the evidence put forward by the honourable member for Holton, demonstrating the excellent transport links enjoyed by Netley Hospital, make a compelling case for the new mid-West Region maternity unit to be located there?'

I looked up at the array of local journalists I had invited to the public gallery and gave a happy wave.

The decision to build the new unit at Netley was confirmed by letter within a week, with a scrawled note from the Secretary of State offering thanks for 'helping resolve a difficult decision' and paying tribute to 'your tireless work for your own constituents and for this government'. Courtesy of Adam's girlfriend at the South Gloucs Gazette, 'tireless work secures new wing for Netley' graced the front page, along with a photo of me giving a thumbs up with a group of beaming nurses.

As expected, another note found its way to my office desk soon afterwards – a note on old, yellow, dusty paper.

'Splendid stuff, dear boy. Plenty more to come. In the meantime, you should celebrate. Wine, women and song, eh?
Maurice

A thought that had been humming somewhere in my chest for weeks took wing. 'Emily, would you like to come for tea on the terrace?'

June gave an audible tut.

Emily looked to Rachel, who bit her lip and carried on typing.

An awkward silence filled the office. 'I mean we should all go. To celebrate our success with the maternity unit. Champagne on me! Maybe some of those little cakes as well.'

June shifted in her seat. Cakes were her meth.

I pressed my advantage. 'Come, I insist. Let's go right now. Close the office. It's an order, comrades.'

It was 3 pm on a Friday, ahead of the late May bank holiday weekend. No one made of flesh and blood could resist the chance to clock off early. Or those made of iron, resentment and lily of the valley eau de toilette. June got up and got her coat.

The terrace is a heavenly place, all the more so in the heavenly month of May. The Thames runs by it, sparkling in the sun. The warm stone of the Palace rears above the tables, glowing with hues of cream and honey. A faint breeze wafts from the east, carrying with it the faint sounds of Westminster Bridge – buses, tourist chatter and the drone of bagpiping buskers. The distant bustle serves only to pleasurably remind you of how calm, comfortable and leisured your current situation is. Achingly polite men and women in green and white uniforms bring you cold beer and colder wine. While the rest of Parliament modernises, the terrace remains a redoubt of Victorian values, imperial comfort and aristocratic lethargy.

I ordered cake, and ice-cold white wine, and we talked of trivialities. June left with the last of the cake. 'Mummy's gone,' said Rachel, opening a packet of cigarettes. The talk moved to boyfriends, past and present. Rachel's was developing along time-honoured lines, from holiday, to meeting the 'parentals', to moving in together. Her pony liked him, and that was the important thing. Emily's boyfriend was – mercifully – receding into the past, a victim of a disastrous decision to go backpacking together. After a month of limited showering and excessive sweating, Aaron and the trip were done.

Emily turned her brown eyes upon me and in a kind sort of voice said, 'How about you, Mr Wilkes? You must have a lovely lady tucked away somewhere?'

'Oh no, nothing to report on that front.'

Rachel pressed home her advantage. 'There must be someone, sir. I know so little about that side of your life. I know it's a bit cheeky, but can I ask?'

I nodded, expecting the inevitable.

'Are you gay, sir?' It's just a lot of people round here are, and, well, you don't ever seem to mention girls.'

I trotted out the polished answer, honed through 800 questions with colleagues, local activists and my mother. 'Wish I was, but I am not. I'm just very busy – married to my work really. Politics is a 24/7 business, if you do it right. And I want to do it right.'

Rachel leaned back in her chair. 'I do understand.' I could see what she understood – boss repressed, even to himself.

It was probably the wine, but I felt a sudden urge to make them understand. To ensure Emily understood.

'I am flesh and blood, I do, um, want things. It's just from the age of 17 my life has been politics. Dad made me join the Young Conservatives in school – it isn't the sexiest look. Same all the way through university. No one wants to date the guy handing out leaflets about tax policy.'

Emily offered me a cigarette. I lit it, trying to look suave, calm and collected, despite my shaking hands.

'Work was the same. Ten hours a day working as a land agent for one of Dad's friends, evening spent stuffing envelopes, weekends on doorsteps. I worked to get here, with every hour I had. There just wasn't time.'

'And now?' Emily asked.

'Where would I go to meet women? I am an MP. If I go on a dating app, it will be in the papers. If I go to a bar, I'll just be another creep. Being single is just part of the job. It's fine. It's the job.'

Rachel said that it seemed very sad, and that we needed more drink. She went inside to get some, leaving Emily and I alone. The terrace was very quiet, with most MPs in their constituencies. Just one other table was occupied, by a peer dozing in the late afternoon sun.

'Mr Wilkes?'

'Yes, Emily.'

'I think you are wonderful. Any girl would be lucky to date you.'

I was at that stage of drunkenness when living according to normal life, normal rules, seemed a gross affront. The mists in my head were drifting in one direction only. It was as fitting, and inevitable, as my next drink. To not do it would be an insult against the wine, an obscenity against that golden evening.

I kissed her. Her lips tasted of nicotine, with a hint of strawberry lip-gloss.

Chapter 6

'There is something wrong in Holton.'

I broke my daydreaming and gave Reggie my full attention for the first time since our meeting began.

Reggie was a pale, nervous man of indeterminate age. As long as I had known him, he had been a boring, if essential, cog in the wheezing machine that was Holton and District Conservative Party. Branch secretary, election agent, repeat candidate for hopeless wards – he had done it all, and all for pathetically little reward. Weekend after weekend spent leafleting, evening after evening trapped behind committee tables, always a single ticket to the Christmas dinner. He had no ambition to be elected, no ambition to be known, no ambition even to be thanked.

It is the Reggies of the world who keep the lights of democracy burning and keep sex shops in business.

He sensed my sudden attention and grew flustered.

'It's Mayor Ainsworth. You know the meetings, eh, the Council meetings. In the chamber. They have gone wrong.'

The latest shit task I had assigned to Reggie was to monitor meetings of Holton Town Council, and to report anything of interest back to me directly. I didn't trust a single one of the councillors to keep me informed. Reggie, as I knew he would, leapt at the chance to do something dutiful and to grab a few hours away from the screaming blankness that was his home life.

The office phone rang in the other room. Reggie looked startled.

'Go on, Reggie.'

'Sorry, sorry. Yes. Mayor Ainsworth. It's the seagulls.'

'The seagulls, Reggie?'

'Yes – the Mayor is obsessed with them. He wants to wipe them out, every one. He has reallocated every budget to pest control and has designated Church Field as a mass burial pit. He calls it the Gull Golgotha.'

'Gosh. How are the other councillors taking it?'

'The Mayor, um, he has a lot of power. No one is prepared to challenge him.'

This did make sense. Holton Town Council was a finely balanced mess of factions, the allotment holders, the shopkeepers, the Britain in Bloom brigade, which has been engaged in an unceasing war for primacy for decades – until Ainsworth turned up. A retired general, returning from long service abroad, he had swiftly won broad support, having the cardinal blessing from each faction of not being part of the 'other lot'. He had kept an uneasy peace, uniting the gangs behind their burning desire not to see their rivals in charge, and a shared ambition to prevent any new building within a five mile perimeter of the town. With this crusade won, he had clearly found another.

'Seagulls? Really?'

'He says they are outsiders, and they come in from Bristol. Ruining the area apparently.'

'Of course they are.'

I called Adam in from the other room, and he arrived bearing biscuits. Homemade, and delicious. Prig.

'Adam, you are the font of all local knowledge. Mayor Ainsworth and the seagulls. What's going on?'

'Ah yes, the great purge. Rumour has it, he has gone a bit doddery. You know he fought in Korea? He is much older than he looks. Plus he has been over-exerting himself lately. Affair with the Town Clerk's wife.'

Adam offered Reggie another biscuit.

Through a mouthful of crumbs, Reggie added that Ainsworth had been spending a lot of time in the Mayor's Parlour with Mrs Clerk, with the door locked and Verdi's operas on full blast. Adultery is the binding glue of politics in Holton.

I refused Adam's second biscuit. 'Your girlfriend at the South Gloucs Gazette, she must be all over this, surely?'

Adam gave a small, wry smile. 'Mr Ainsworth is on the board.'

'So the Council won't move and the Gazette won't report it?'

'Well, the councillors are pretty unhappy and worried, but no, they won't do anything about it. Each faction is far too worried about its rival winning the vacated Mayor's seat. Gazette staff won't touch this with a barge pole – a staffing review is due to be considered by the board in the autumn.'

I felt my interest wane, and filed the matter as diverting, but pointless.

'Looks like there are going to be a lot of dead seagulls in Holton.' Adam gave a jocular laugh, and Reggie squeaked along.

I faked an important phone call with the Farming Minister, ushered them out and returned to daydreaming. Daydreaming about her.

Prurient reader, becalm your indignation, bestill your stirrings.

Emily and I only kissed that night on the Terrace. A sweet, lingering kiss, but a kiss alone. Followed by sweet, stilted conversation when Rachel returned from the toilet, followed by a goodbye at the entrance to the tube where she slipped her number nimbly into my hand, followed by texting. Lots of texting.

Enquiring texts, happy texts, texts of gifs 'to keep you entertained when you are in the boring country'. It had only been a week, but already I had more texts from her on my phone than from every other contact combined. Smiley faces had given way to shy x's, to multiple x's. We hadn't directly addressed that moment on the Terrace, but it lay behind every message. The number of texts was escalating. Things were escalating. This was the second-best thing that had ever happened to me, only narrowly behind getting elected.

I looked at her latest message 'Good luck with your meetings today you amazing person (smiley face emoji, clover leaf emoji, three xxx's), felt the happiness pulse and wondered on further escalation.

In addition to questioning the ethics of a man in his thirties daydreaming about a 19 year old, you may also be asking how an elected representative of the people – one of the besuited ones, endlessly busy meeting the demands of a modern, 24-hour democracy – could have time for it. Truth is, being an MP is a little like being a vicar. If you want, if you are an upstanding and dedicated fulfiller of a vocation, you can choose to fill every minute with good causes, helping the needy and mopping up after the sick. If, however, like me, you are in the game because you like having some initials after your name and swaddling the thinness of your soul with the blanket of tradition and the duvet of belonging, you can get away with doing very, very little. Turn up at the right time, get noticed doing so, talk about how busy you are – done. The majority of MPs are in the former category. I and other cunts are in the latter.

That day, I had just one other appointment in the diary. I wasn't due for another five hours, so went back to my Holton flat to 'work on some papers'. I drank 4 beers, sent 14 texts to Emily and worked on a pleasing email to June, highlighting to her that she had sent an email on my behalf asking about legislative timetables not to SLSC (Statutory Liaison Lords Committee) but to the SLSC (South London Swimming Club).

I was in an excellent mood, albeit torn between 'you have thrown me in at the deep end' or 'it's unacceptably slap-splash' as an email sign-off, by the time Adam picked me up in his car. We drove through the setting sun to a new housing estate outside Pilford, distinguished by a particularly virulent shade of red–purple brick. Mr Wiggins was waiting for us, with an entourage of employees and photographers.

Mr Wiggins was a local builder, an old crony of my father's. Together with a handful of other red-cheeked, brass-bottomed local businessmen they had ridden the post-war Bristol building boom together – squabbling, boasting and drinking over their profits. For reasons lost in a cloud of Trundles Best Bitter, my father had always referred to him as 'old Cumgizzard'. Cumgizzard had had the last laugh, surviving my father and naming a spectacularly ugly block of flats after 'that old rogue, his protégé'. Cumgizzard had invited me to visit his latest development and I endured the usual tour round the identikit houses. The architect took great pride in informing me that the zinc roofs and purple bricks 'reflected the local vernacular and the deep red soil of Devon'. When I reminded him that Devon was 80 miles away, and that slate was the traditional Gloucestershire roofing material, he muttered that laymen never could understand art. We had an obligatory ribbon-cutting photo in the fading light and then we were in for what Cumgizzard described as a 'real treat' – badger watching.

The new development had bulldozed over a meadow and part of an ancient wood, obliterating a badger sett in the process. As Cumgizzard's pet ecologist explained, they had created a new home for the badgers, using the very best materials. Cumgizzard proudly added that the development would be known as 'Badger Drive', 'so everyone knows this is an eco-friendly development'. The ecologist, with dread-locks and hand tattoos left over from a life before he sold out, made a strange, desperate noise and stared at his shoes. The very best materials turned out to be some clay pipes stuck into a hole, in a boggy bit of ground unsuitable for building, around which some slender, doomed aspen trees had been scattered around, still in their nursery pots. We all lay down on a groundsheet and waited for the badgers. Darkness came, cold came, cramp came, but no badgers. After 30 minutes, Cumgizzard suggested 'maybe they are out playing over there' – he flung his arm out to the west. The orange fuzz of road lamps and the drone of traffic on the M5 answered back. 'Or maybe over there.' From the north came the barking of dogs, and muffled shots. Alfie Dalton's land.

After ten more agonising minutes, I felt a tap on my shoulder. I looked round, hoping Adam had come up with an excuse for me to leave. It was Maurice, wrapped up in what looked like an old army overcoat. He crooked his finger at me. I said I had to make an urgent call. Cumgizzard grunted. No one looked round as I rose to my feet.

Maurice leaned into my ear. 'Come, the air is thin here.' We trudged away from the development, into the deep darkness, and far out of earshot. We stopped in a place where I could feel wet grass around my feet, and hear the gurgle of a spring.

Maurice sniffed and gave a satisfied sigh. 'That's better – we are back in the old lands now. Tales are still breathing here, thick as cream.'

He held up his hand, and a warm yellow light trickled around us. I could see him properly now, replete in a huge khaki jacket with a fur trim, and galoshes that went to his thighs. He saw me looking.

'When in the country, dress for the country. How have you been, boy?'

'Well, still haunted by you.'

One of his bone-shaking laughs.

'But I should thank you, that hospital stunt worked. Really well.'

'More to come, boy, much more to come. This Holton Town Council business, for example; there is an opportunity there.'

'What do you mean?'

'Young Ainsworth, the mad mayor. I knew his father – always was a dash of the cuckoo in that family. French blood, I believe.'

'So you have heard about the seagulls. Your sources are impressive, for a dead man.'

The light from his hand ceased and we were plunged into darkness. The night suddenly seemed very black and very quiet.

'I am sorry, continue. I want to hear about this opportunity.'

The light came again and Maurice continued. 'Ainsworth's obsession will run Holton into the ground. You can stop it and gain a lot of credit by doing so. Great successes in the country have a way of resounding in town, if whispered in the right ears.'

'The man is all-powerful in Holton, I can't take him on. I can't fix brains either. How am I meant to stop him spending every penny on slaughtering seagulls?'

'Two words, boy: Baverstock Falconer.'

With that, the light – and Maurice – disappeared.

I spent a minute calling his name in vain, before accepting he had actually gone. The night seemed very dark again. I craved living, breathing humans – even old Cumgizzard.

I splashed, slipped and groped my way along a hedgerow, till eventually I found them. The man himself saw the mud up my trousers and asked if I had gone dogging – 'like your old dad'. His acolytes cackled. We lay in the cold for what seemed like an eternity, until we saw some furtive movements amid the pit. It was dark, but to me it looked a lot like a rat nibbling on a discarded sandwich. Cumgizzard declared victory, saying it was a badger 'happy as a sandboy in his shiny new home', and we – at last – were allowed to leave.

The next day was a Saturday, and unusually busy. I spent the afternoon buried in the county archives at Holton Library and, after few phone calls, made my way to Holton Town Hall for the 6 pm Council meeting. Reggie sat by me in the public galley, wearing one of his 'wacky ties for the weekend' (purple dolphins, playing the trombone, on a vomit-green ocean). The Town Hall was a glorious building, built in high Victorian pomp of Holton, all turrets and marble on the outside, rococo plaster panelling on the inside. Holton's coat of arms was emblazoned on every available surface – a black dog rearing up on a blue background, teeth bared, ready to rip the throat out of anyone without disposable income.

The town councillors drifted in groups, faction by faction, glaring at their rivals, whispering to each other and shuffling their papers. Silence fell as Mayor Ainsworth strode in, resplendent in a pinstripe suit – with a red rose in his lapel and the gold chains of office draped around his neck. He was a tall, well-built man, with a mane of white hair, an aquiline nose and blazing blue eyes. Energy crackled from his every pore.

'Good evening, gentlemen. I declare this meeting of Holton Town Council open.' His was a voice made for parade grounds.

'Minutes from last time – any objections? I take your silence as consent. Isn't that right, Mr Clerk?'

The poor cuckolded town clerk, a small man in glasses, gave a sad smile before returning to typing.

'Right, agenda item one – the gardening budget. Have you all read my paper?'

Lots of eager nodding from the councillors.

'Well, I have written another one, a better one.' He threw a sheaf of papers across the table.

'It proposes a shift in priorities, to reflect the nuisance that now plagues us.'

One of the councillors put his head in his hands.

Ainsworth started moving his hands up and down, very fast. 'The gulls! The flying vermin, the cursed ones. Thousands of sharp-beaked city thugs, defacing our town, defecating on our prides, pecking at our joys. The gulls!'

The last two words came out in a shriek. He paused to wipe spittle from the corner of his mouth.

'I propose that the gardening budget be redirected, to respond to this horrid threat. The time for action is now, gentlemen.'

A female councillor, undaunted by the repeat reference to gentlemen, raised a hand to ask what would happen to the three gardeners the town council employed – 'surely we can't make these public servants redundant?'

Ainsworth snorted. 'No, no, no, dear lady. They shall not be fired – they shall be retrained. As marksmen! Yes, yes, they shall be issued with shotguns and let loose upon the feathered scum. A bonus for every ten heads they bring in! Oh, they shall garden, they shall garden death!'

The woman, who appeared to be head of the Britain in

Bloom faction, bravely raised her hand again. 'I feel I must raise an objection. To cease all gardening work is to give up on any chance of winning a prize next year. This would be the first year since 1976' – she gestured to a groaning trophy cabinet – 'that Holton has not brought home a decoration. Such an eventuality would devastate each and every household in our town.'

An allotment gang member piped up. 'Not mine.'

Ainsworth directed a wolfish smile at Britain in Bloom woman.

'Dear lady, may I remind you that the gardening budget is the largest we have? And that, when we agreed an unprecedented rise last year, you assured this council that it would be used for the good of the town, and not to advance narrow interests, such as your own floristry business? Should we look to reallocate resources to support more public-minded civic projects?'

Britain in Bloom woman scribbled furiously but did not put her hand back up. A man, who I recognised as head of the Allotments Federation, stood up and started mumbling about the benefits to public health of more money for cabbage growing.

Ainsworth cut him off sharply. 'Enough of that, tight agenda to get through. Now, my new paper – let's avoid a vote if possible, horrible divisive things, aren't they? Any objections to my proposal?'

A nanosecond passed.

'No, excellent. The gardeners start at the range on Monday, live ammunition issued on Tuesday. Should nab a couple of hundred by Friday. Das Aldertag!'

He smashed his fist down on the council table, shaking coffee cups and dislodging a monocle from the eye of one of the more ancient councillors.

'Now – item two. Hamworthy Infants School. It will not

have escaped your notice that this has become a gathering place for delinquents after hours.'

Concerned looks around the council table. Someone suggested that the police should be contacted.

Another fist slam from Ainsworth. 'Feathered undesirables! The spawn of the winged Beezlebub, writing and cawing all over the roof. It's disgusting and it needs to be cleansed. Gentlemen, you will be relieved to know that I have a plan.'

Reggie gave a nervous cough beside me.

'We use the depraved predictions of the enemy against them. They like the flat roof of the school – let them enjoy it, for eternity.' The last word was spat out, like an owl expelling a pellet. 'We shall lace loaves of bread with arsenic, lay them out on the roof, and let gluttony do the rest.'

The allotment king raised his hand. 'Arsenic is a powerful chemical. The school is within 100 metres of the Hamworthy plots – wind could carry it over and infect the ground. Dreadful for growing, fatal for legumes. Probably not very good for the school pupils either.'

Ainsworth waved his hand in dismissal. 'Nonsense, exposure to chemicals is good for children – toughens their immune systems up. All my toys as a child were made of lead, didn't do me any harm.'

Reggie gave a small, strangled noise.

Ainsworth swung round to glare at us, then continued. 'The sprogs can use the bodies for dissection, that should spice up biology lessons, eh? Of course, we will leave some corpses on the roof. Pour encourager les autres.'

He looked at the clock. 'Time for a break, I think. Motion carried! Have you got that, clerk?'

The clerk gave another sad nod.

'Capital – I shall need you working late tonight to get the arsenic supplies ordered at once. I am happy to keep your good wife company until you are finished. All part of the service. Right, we reconvene in five minutes, gentlemen.'

He stalked off to the Mayor's parlour, giving the clerk a manly slap on the back as he went.

This was my chance – I followed him in.

The Parlour was a small wood-panelled room, crammed with portraits of mayors past, two chaise longues, a gramophone and a very well-stocked drinks cabinet. A model of a sailing ship took pride of place in front of the one window – Holton's contribution to the war effort (rather than contribute a spitfire, or something similarly practical/vulgar, the town had insisted on paying for a yacht for admirals to relax in). A pair of tossed knickers hung from one spar.

Ainsworth was surprised to see me. 'Wilkins, isn't it, the Parliamentary wallah? What on earth do you want?'

'It's Wilkes, Mr Mayor – we met at the remembrance service last year.'

He jerked his head towards the chaise longues. I perched on the one that looked the least damp.

'Mr Mayor, I first of all wanted to thank you for all your work in Holton. It has been noticed on-high, and is appreciated.'

Flattery always, always works. Ainsworth visibly defrosted.

'This seagull work is particularly great to see. We need more men of vision, willing to tackle issues that have been ignored for too long.'

'Quite right.' He leaned forward conspiratorially. 'I say, do you think you could get the PM to do a speech about the sky-maggots? The declaration of a nationwide purge would do wonders. Really get them on the run.'

'I will look into that, Mr Mayor, fear not. In the meantime, I wanted to raise another proposition with you. Have you heard of the Baverstock Falconer?

'Can't say I have.'

'Well, it's one of those funny old titles – medieval in origin. Started at Baverstock Castle, when the Earl Lennard ran everything here.'

'Better days.'

I nodded encouragingly.

'Well, the falconer was a very important aide to the Earl. As well as running his hunting, he also helped him keep the peace, fighting for him on occasion. The title would only go to a local gentleman of proven worth and reputation. Often a gentleman from nearby Holton.'

Ainsworth's eyes gleamed. The fish was on the hook.

'The last falconer was appointed in 1711; the role fell into abeyance after that. You know how these old traditions die.'

Ainsworth grunted. 'Bloody incomers.'

'Exactly. But there is good news – the new Earl Lennard, young Johnny – do you know him? He wants to bring the position back. And he wants you to do it.'

It had been an afternoon well spent. The archives had all the details of the old position, and I had the phone number of the Earl – a Tory donor, mad keen to get on the Conservatives' candidate list himself. A quick phone call had ensured that Johnny understood that, in return for re-establishing the position and offering it to Ainsworth, I would drip gentle words into important ears.

I salted the hook with crack.

'You see, the thing about the position is that it needs a man with a track record to do it – and someone who has dignity. The role comes with a suite of rooms in one of the towers at Baverstock Castle, and ceremonial duties every Whitsun, blowing a horn and wearing a big hat, that sort of thing.'

'Is there other renumeration?' Ainsworth asked.

'Oh yes – a stipend of £40,000 a year. Although given

that you would be living rent free in the castle, I am not sure you really want for cash. Oh, and you get the right to be buried with full honours in the Lennard chapel at Gloucester Cathedral.'

Ainsworth was positively licking his lips by now. 'This is all very flattering, but what about my work here?'

'That's the beauty – you could carry on with your important work combatting the seagull menace. What's the core job of a falconer?'

'Releasing birds of prey on vermin.'

'Exactly! You can keep Baverstock Castle free of seagulls, set an example to the rest of us. Great things could come from that. Why you could even put seagull heads over the gate, like they used to do with traitors in the Middle Ages.'

Eyes shining, Ainsworth accepted the position.

The scheme was complete within an hour. Ainsworth accepted on the condition that he had to start the role that very night, to show his commitment. He gave a brief resignation statement to the town council, before throwing his mayoral chain on the table and stalking out to buy a new gun and hop in a taxi to Baverstock. Pandemonium briefly reigned, with the different factions putting in six different proposals for a new chair, to six deadlocked votes.

I stepped in, as 'an impartial authority, keen to resolve this difficult situation, for the town we all love'. I recognised the need for a chair 'capable of rising above the fray – a clean skin, acceptable to all'. I suggested that we had 'the perfect candidate, sitting in this very room now', a 'local man, content to serve, and with no ambition to dictate'.

To his shock, Reggie was co-opted as Mayor by a unanimous vote. With shaking hands, he wiped the nervous sweat from his lip, tightened his purple dolphin tie and put on the chains of office.

Chapter Seven

The week after, back in Westminster, I was given a welcome sign that my political stock was rising. We were voting on a Bill to adjust pensions tax rules, something that would save the government money while leaving 'the bottom six quintiles net neutral by the fourth quarter'. No one understood the details, but the government was for it and opposition against, so both sides whirled through their great dance. As the Chief Whip was ushering us into the Aye Lobby, smiling like a sheepdog barking his flock onto the abattoir van, he winked at me. I looked back in surprise and he winked again.

Bowels churning, I walked back to him. 'Is everything ok, sir?'

'Very ok, Mr Wilkes.' He had remembered my name. This was either very good, or very bad.

'You know, little Wilkes, a little birdie in a little town told me something about you.'

'Good I hope?'

'Oh, very good. I understand you sorted a little problem. Removed a dangerous lunatic, while maintaining peace among the natives. Very impressive.'

'Thank you, sir.'

'What with this success and your hospital triumph, your

stock is rising, Mr Wilkes. Keep it up, and I might just mention you to the PM.'

I was whirled on by a new surge of MPs keen to display their conspicuous loyalty by walking very purposefully into the Aye Lobby, as close to the eyes of the Chief Whip as they could manage.

It later transpired that his wife was the niece of the leader of the Britain in Bloom gang on Holton Town Council. She had never mentioned the relationship to me or anyone else as, in classic Holton style, she thought the Chief Whip a little common (born in Sheffield, villa in Spain, watches football).

I was on a high for the next new few days, breezing along on dreams of Ministerial office, until Rachel conjured up a cloud for my blue horizon. I had been in the office, joking with Emily and exchanging looks that went on a little too long, when Rachel had asked when she could write the piece on Parliamentary ghosts that she had been researching. I said I had studied the subject further and felt that the piece was probably not needed any more. Rachel typed very fast for a while, before breaking her silence to invite Emily to drinks that night, adding 'a really cute guy is coming'. Blood. Veins. Ice. I waited with a rising pulse for the invite to be extended to me. It was not. I had spent much of the morning pondering whether I could, in all propriety, invite Emily for a 'just us' drink that night. Damned, dallying, dithering Wilkes.

It was as a result of this that I found myself alone on a table in Portcullis House at 11 pm that Thursday. The route from the researchers favoured bar, the Undercroft (sticky carpets, name dropping and hormones) to the exit ran through Portcullis and by stationing myself there I was sure to be able to spot Emily as she left. I had no clear plan as to what to do when I saw her. I just needed to see if she was leaving in tow with some chisel-jawed rugby thug, ten years younger, ten times stronger, ten times posher than me. I could not stay at home speculating. I had to see.

I had brought some papers with me to look busy and I alternated between reading the same sentences over and over and checking my phone. Last message from her received at 7.10 pm, no reply to mine sent at 7.14 pm.

I was just typing out, deleting, then typing again a 'how's it going' text, when I heard someone call my name. I looked up, hoping to see her. The vast atrium of Portcullis was empty, the tables that resounded with the clatter of hasty lunches and the sift and suck of gossip during the day were still and silent, waiting for politics to breathe again in the morning. A light flickered in the closed café next to me.

I heard my name again. It seemed to be coming from above. I looked up.

He was gliding straight through the glass roof, in full black tie, a huge evening cloak billowing like a parachute around him, like some mutant, terrible partridge descending to its nest. Down he came, down past the wooden girders holding up the ceiling, down past the fig trees imported at great cost to oxygenate the air, down onto the fountains built to hide political indiscretions behind the soft gurgle of water.

He rose from the waters, a horrible cross between the phantom of the opera and the Venus de Milo, and walked over to my table looking smug.

'Always wanted to do that.' He looked contemptuously at a plastic no smoking sign on the table. 'Ghastly place this, wouldn't have happened in my time.'

I looked at his regalia, from bow tie, to buttonhole red rose and the medal ribbons on his ample chest. 'Why are you in evening dress, Maurice?'

'Off to a ghosts and ghoulies ball on the Cutty Sark.

Great fun. Dusty violins, faded velvet, the full danse maca-
bre. Sometimes we take the boat on the Thames and out
along the Kent marshes. Terrifies the coastguard.'

He gave one of his horrid chuckles and I decided not to
ask for any more details.

'Anyway, boy, why are you skulking here tonight? Bright
young thing like you should be out on the town.'

He clapped his hand to his head before I could answer.
'Of course – her. Piece of advice, boy: don't piss gad about.
Swift, decisive, manly action, that's the ticket.'

He gave a leery wink. 'Anyway, down to business. Things
are going well, don't you think?'

'Yes, they are. Thank you for your, um, help.'

'Pleasure is all mine. And soon to be yours, if you keep
following my advice.' Another wink.

I reminded myself I was in his debt, that he was one of
the walking dead – and that he seemed to have power over
events. 'I am very grateful for all your help. What would
you like me to do next? On the politics front, I mean.'

'I don't want you to do anything, boy. I might suggest something. Up to you as to whether you do it or not.
Although I would hope that, after all our successes so far,
you may have grown to trust me a little.'

'Yes, yes, of course,' I said.

'Capital. Well, here it is then. The M17a.'

'The road?'

'Yes, the road that is going to wipe out 50 hectares of
prime farmland in your constituency. It's a travesty. But also
an opportunity. The hospital and town council triumphs
have built you up – this is the one that is going to take you
over the line.'

'Over the line?'

'Over the door and under the table. Cabinet table.'

Unexpectedly he gave a deep, retching gasp – like a trout

on a river bank. He doubled over, choking. Just as I was wondering how best perform the Heimlich manoeuvre on a man already long dead, he stamped his foot twice. That seemed to put him back in control and he stood up again, buttonhole rose askew.

'Damn building. Too modern. Air too bloody thin. I haven't got long – where was I?'

'The M17a.'

'That's the one. Well, think creatively. You want feet under the Cabinet table. The road is to go over your turf. Couldn't it go under?' His hand dived down, then rose up again. I found the gesture disturbingly sexual.

I suddenly grasped his meaning. 'You mean a tunnel? Underground? Is that possible? I suppose a tunnel would create jobs. People like the Channel Tunnel.'

'Talking of under, your tie is sticking out of your flies. Not very statesmanlike, boy.'

I looked down and hurriedly fixed it. I looked up, and of course the fucker was gone.

Just then I saw Emily out of the corner of my eye, walking across the other side of the atrium to the main exit. She was indisputably, wonderfully alone, looking down at her phone and typing hard. Right on cue my phone pinged.

'Evening all right thanks, but not as fun as when you are there.' Tongue out emoji.

She passed out onto the street without seeing me. My heart sang. My head pondered swift, manly and decisive action.

I spent the next morning studying a map of my constituency. The M5, which carries traffic from the Midlands down into Bristol like chips down the gullet of seagull, slices to the left of the constituency boundary, hitting the M17 just on the western edge of Pilford. There the gut twists, with traffic greasing its way along the M17 from London to the

West Country hitting the north–south stream. A series of complicated loops had been built in the 1970s to govern flow and counter flow, succeeding only in making the tortured mess of car and concrete multi-storey.

In this Minotaur's maze of roads, different streams of England meet and despise each other – the family from Bromsgrove in their caravan bound for Dawlish, the couple from Esher riding the Jag down to their place in Padstow, the lorry driver bearing 40 tonnes of pig shit from Hereford to the Port of Bristol. There they stew, panic and beep horns. If you stand in the right street in Pilford, you can feel the stress from half a mile away – and smell the fevered Greggs-Steak-Bake breath.

Cabinet Ministers tend to spend quite a bit of time in Jags trying to reach Padstow, so the problem of the M5–M17 interchange had been noted in London. Noted and subjected to three infrastructure reviews, two scoping papers and one manifesto promise. My Party had pledged to 'resolve the North Bristol bottleneck and invest in South West roads on a scale not seen since the Industrial Revolution'. Given that no records existed of early 19th century spending on roads, it was safe ground to stand on.

The latest and most well-received scoping paper had suggested the 'M17a' as a decisive cut through the tangle. The new road would branch out of the M5 well north of Bristol, slicing down my constituency and across the M17a into the city. The idea was this spur would isolate, contain and transport Midlands–Bristol traffic, helping free up roadway for the Jags heading west. The cost – 50 hectares of lost fields, woods and hedges. Horror at this prospect united Holton, Netley and Pilford, and I had duly spent the past two years publicly rubbishing the plan, while inwardly resigned to its inevitability. While my constituents believed that another way of resolving the bottleneck could be found, and I encouraged them in that belief, I knew the balance. The familiarity of a road solution, the chance to present it as 'infrastructure delivery, investing in our long-term economic plan for GREAT Britain', plus the prospect of Kensington to Padstow in less than four hours, was politically irresistible. The churn of concrete sounds louder than the squeak of a fieldmouse.

I looked at the map for a long time, trying to work out how Maurice thought a tunnel would help. A tunnel under the Severn Estuary? Pointless, expensive and bound to provoke tedious discussion about Welsh devolution. A tunnel to widen the M5 roadway at the most congested part? Would undermine the foundations of hundreds of homes, shaking house prices and slashing the Conservative vote. Then I saw it. A small black line, running through the out-skirts of Pilford, where the gap between the M5 and M17 was at its narrowest. It was an old railway, built in the 19th century to carry Gloucestershire milk and cheese to the bel-lies of Bristol workers, axed by Beeching in the 60s, used by dog walkers and flashers ever since. Surely a tunnel could go under that without harming any homes? It wouldn't even have to be a long tunnel – the distance between the M5 and M17 at that point couldn't be more than a mile. Only one spot of green lay on the line, a small block of woodland marked on the map as 'Boars Copse'. No one would mind too much about one scrap of woodland, would they?

Christ, this could work.

A weekend of calls, googling and typing. My paper was ready on Monday morning and by Monday afternoon I was in the office of Mary Miles. As my whip, Mary was the most important person I knew would agree to meet with me. Even then it was marginal, only my 'I have something confidential to tell you' had secured the slot in her diary.

She looked at me over her desk, eyebrows drawn, a

prosecutor at the top of her game cross-examining a knicker thief.

'Well, what do you have to tell me, Wilkes? What have you been up to? What mess do you want to fix?'

'No mess, Mary, promise – I have an idea to propose.'

'Look, if you have been diddling anyone, snorting anything or putting sex toys on your expenses, it's better to tell me now.' She gave me a long stare. 'Even if it's something really disgusting. Fess up, take your punishment like a man and let me sort the rest.'

I looked at the Churchill print behind her, framed by two Union Jacks. A bulldog statue sat on her desk, next to a large pen in the shape of a cigar and a spitfire paperweight. There were lots of Churchill freaks in Parliament, but I hadn't realised she was one. I trimmed to the wind.

'I have got an idea – something bold, best of British. A buccaneering proposal to get round pettifogging bureaucracy and achieve something, just like the old days, before Europe and red tape ruined it all.'

She didn't thaw. 'Well get to it then. I have been hearing surprisingly good things about you from the Chief Whip. Don't ruin it by dicking around.'

'The M17a issue, Mary. I can solve it.'

'You may be surprised to learn, Wilkes, that I do not have an encyclopaedic knowledge of every road in your flea-bitten constituency. Elucidate.'

'It's a road extension, over greenfield, designed to reduce congestion around Bristol. Promised in the manifesto. Will lose me 2,000 votes – and the Party my seat.'

'Your sacrifice will not be forgotten. You shall give your tomorrow, so that commuters can have their today, and we can pick up new seats elsewhere.'

'Well that's the thing. I think I have the solution to pick up the new seats and retain mine.'

'Bully for you.'

'It's a tunnel, Mary. A short, cheap tunnel, that builds the road, saves the greenfield and reduces congestion.'

She picked up her cigar-pen and started writing. I decided this was a good sign.

'You see, I have found a much shorter route, which can all be tunnelled. It's cheaper than the long road, won't create any greenfield issues – or building issues – and will create more jobs than a traditional road.'

She looked up sharply. 'How much cheaper?'

Thankfully, I was prepared. 'I have spoken to old Cumgizzard – a local builder – and he says the cost per square metre works out £16 cheaper with a tunnel. The tunnel route goes over cheap, marginal ground, owned by the council. They are desperate for cash and will sell quick and low.'

'Good to see that our local government competitiveness policies are bearing fruit.'

'Oh yes. They will settle for any price. The tunnel gets built, congestion gets relieved, my constituency stays true. It a win, win, win. I just need the Minister to back it as the best option.'

Mary leaned back in her chair and waved her cigar-pen at me. Churchill directing the Battle of the Atlantic.

'Is it a British building company? Local jobs to deliver the tunnel? British concrete? British sandwiches in the building canteen?'

'Oh yes, all very local.'

She balanced the cigar-pen on the bulldog paperweight, in a decisive manner.

'Right, get an adjournment debate. I'll get some deadwood in for you, so you will have some friendly company. If the wonks at the Department for Transport find your claims hold up, you will get Ministerial backing. If they don't, you will get ripped apart. Eviscerated in front of your peers. Wormfood. Deal?'

'Yes, Mary – and thank you.'

'Good. That's us then, you can see yourself out.'

I backed out, nodding repeated thanks.

'Oh, and Wilkes?'

'Yes?'

'If you must wank in public toilets, don't get caught.'

Thank you, Mary.

Chapter 8

It was a sparkling June day. White light and the sound of London in holiday mood seeped in from the stained-glass windows of the pub, kept at a respectful distance by heavy purple curtains. Inside all was dark, cool wood and the calm, imperial ticking of a grandfather clock. The Cross Keys had stood since the time of Gladstone, shielded from the world by two more garish pubs on either side and a tiny, heavily curtained frontage. The casual eye passed over the pub, dismissing it as a strange, private place. The connoisseur relished it as such.

Undisturbed by the vulgarities of popular demand, the place hadn't changed in a century. The mahogany of the bar was still polished to a high sheen, the same stuffed, faded parrot leered drunkenly at a print of King Edward. Deep, ominous onions quietly decayed in pickle glasses, no crisp flavour had been permitted on the premises and no fizz had ever defaced a beer. The wine list was entirely in French and the one whiskey on offer came in a bottle with a tartan-clad man on it, from a firm that stopped producing in 1936.

Narrow your eyes and the outlines of cars beyond the window take on a distinctly coach-like shape. The blur of tourists on the pavement features an unusual number of top hats and high bonnets. The sound of horses on cobblestones resounds. From the Calvary barracks at Horseguards your brain tells you, just before the hairs on the back of your neck remind you that Horeseguards is too far away to be audible.

Emily and I were the only customers, save a clutch of clergyman plotting over port and lemonade in the far corner. A delicious co-occurrence had carried us here: an empty couple of hours in my diary, and a text from her saying she was bored. I saw the opportunity for swift, manly and decisive action and, within a flutter of my stomach, the date was secured. We had met on Whitehall, casting glances behind our backs like eloping lovers, and had hurried into the discreet shelter of the Cross Keys. Once inside, a curious elation washed over us. The rest of Westminster was at work, grinding out emails, boring through committees, and we were at play. Safe from modernity, safe from the world, in this castle of mirth, whose walls had kept out drear, fear and puritans for more than a century.

We worked our way through the three beers on offer, from Hatherley's Best Bitter to Morley's Empire Stout, and back again to our favourite – Arkell's Golden Sunlight. It was England in a glass, the heavy swell of barley, the soaring charge of dancing green hops, the faint lysergic trace of something darker and older from the deepwood.

The hops and the sense of truancy loosened our tongues and we talked, as easily and freely as beer filling a glass. We gossiped about the staff and MPs in the offices next to mine – the disgraced Minister still holding pathetic networking drinks parties to pave a way for a return that would never come, the coked-up researcher who had binged for a week without sleeping, changing clothes, or leaving the Parliamentary estate, and the American intern, drunk for the first time, who had gone home with an octogenarian Lord with shrapnel still in his leg from the Normandy beaches. We joked about June and her annual perfume budget, and speculated as to whether her birthdate was pre- or post-war. Emily even ventured a joke about Rachel's predilection for men who looked and sounded like her father – adding that 'of course, I have nothing against older men either'.

The conversation was veering into dangerous, delicious territory.

'Ah, but Emily, you have your whole life ahead of you. Don't waste it on an elderly, syphilitic sybarite like me.'

She hit my head with a beer mat 'Don't be so silly. You have to have had sex to have syphilis.'

I laughed, in a breezy and confident way that suggested that the thought of me never having had sex was ridiculous.

'Seriously though, young Emily – you have your whole life ahead of you. What do you want to do with it?'

Her eyes darkened by a register. We were on the serious talk now.

'Well, I have got the travelling bug out of my system.'

'And the boyfriend bug with it.'

'Hah, I suppose so. There will be lots of boys to meet at university though.'

I clutched the beer mat, to save being dragged into the icy pit of panic that had opened in my core.

'Yeah, I will tick off university, then a job. Then marriage, babies, a job again. You know, the standard stuff.'

She took another long draw at her beer. 'I think the standard stuff is fine really. People have a go, but it's not a bad deal, is it? Work a few days a week, then have a few days to live as you want – with nice food, nice drink, nice people. Modern life is pretty amazing when you think about it. Duvets, Netflix, four different types of houmous in every supermarket. Yeah, I think that's what I want my life to be. A life full of nice things, a life full of splendid memories. 75% being happy, 25% spreading happiness to others. Does that sound naïve?'

'Not at all.'

Emily smiled. 'It's silly, people hunger for immortality, to be remembered for great things. But living a gentle, nice life, then passing it on – that's true immortality, isn't it? Creating a bit of warmth in this cold world, then giving it to others.'

It was the philosophy I was expecting, typical of her class, and background – self-absorbed but not selfish, careless but not cruel. That background danced before me, in the suds of my glass. A century, maybe two, of comfortable middle-class life, every generation a little more comfortable than the last. Large, brick houses, hunkered down on the healthiest hills of London, thick ivy cleaning the air before it reached a single window, the fence at the bottom of the garden (just beyond the apple orchard, the one that Uncle Hugo planted, where the cricket stumps go in June), keeping out dirt, disease and disgrace. Privileged, sheltered, ferociously innocent.

Emily pointed her finger at me. 'How about you? What are you going to do when you grow up?'

I was without an answer. The catastrophic emptiness of my life roared up to meet me.

'I don't feel grown up. Peter Pan, that's me.'

'Seriously, Robert, do you feel you have anything left to do? I mean, you're in Parliament, that's got to be pretty great, right? You have made it.'

The beer on my tongue and the soft light dappling the table invited confessions. 'For years, all I wanted was to get elected. I spent every day shaking hands, laughing at bad jokes, delivering sodden leaflets, and every night dreaming of what it would be like to win – to walk into the Commons, into all that history and power – and to belong.'

I gulped back more beer. 'But I am here, and I don't belong. Backbenchers are nothing, we belong about as much as the tourists do. No one knows my name, and the few who do see me as just another pathetic try-hard, one of hundreds of faceless fuckers in cheap suits. Bottom feeders, that's what they call us. I have won the race, only to find there is a whole other one to go.'

'So you want to be promoted to be a Minister?' Emily asked.

'To be promoted to anything. You have to keep moving, keep winning, in this game – that's the point.'

'There doesn't seem to be much point to me. It's like you're scrabbling up an escalator, constantly. Must be very tiring. What do you want to do when you get to the top?'

I was preparing a standard political answer about enabling innovation and looking out for the little guy, when she added, 'That's different from what anyone else would do, I mean. Why does it have to be you at the top, and why can you only be happy if it's you?'

Bugger. I scrambled. 'I just want to be there. Always have done.'

She kept pressing. 'It was your dad who made you get into politics, wasn't it?'

'Yes.'

'Why did he do that?'

'It was important to him, to see the family established. He was a self-made man, pulled himself up by his bootstraps and all that. He had a lot of money by the end, but people in the golf club still used to make jokes about using the tradesmen entrance. Having a son as an MP would have shown them I suppose.'

Deep truths flash into drinking sessions like bolts of lightning. This particular truth about my dad reaching out – past the very deep grave they had dug for him, his breached heart and vast gut – to direct the deepest desires of my life to assuage an old golf club grievance was not particularly welcome. I decided to drown it out in more booze.

'That's enough of the deep stuff. I am getting you another drink, before I have to pay you as my therapist.'

We had two more pints of Golden Sunlight and our talk reverted to the little things. Anecdotes, memories, the promise of wonderous newness sparking to life in the shrinking distance between us. At one point my hand rested on the table. She placed hers over it. There it remained, until the grandfather clock at the bar sounded 2 pm.

'Gosh, shouldn't we be going?' Emily said, squeezing my hand in consolation.

'Sadly, tragically, I think we should. You better go first, I will follow in 30 minutes.'

'I'll miss you.'

I leaned forward to kiss her, but she ducked away. She gestured at the clergymen clustered over their port, and then at King Edward eying us beadily above the bar. 'Not in here, it doesn't seem right. Too dusty.'

She dragged me by the hand to the street. There, in the blazing, official light of a Whitehall afternoon, in front of the tourists, the civil servants hurrying sandwiches from Boots to desk, the taxi drivers idling amid the fumes, under the stone spurs of some long dead General, she kissed me.

I watched her walk down the street away from me, breathed in the last of her perfume and relished the sensation of living. Half-remembered lines of poetry sounded in the distance.

Whan that Aprill with his shoures soote
The droghte of March hath perced to the roote,
And bathed every veyne in swich licour

I walked around in a happy, tipsy daze, with half an hour to kill and London stretched benevolently before me. The lions in Trafalgar Square were smiling, their charge atop the column winking. Every stone in the Square radiated drowsy content, every fountain burbled fellowship.

I passed under Admiralty Arch and into the green of St James's Park. The summer hadn't yet parched the grass, and every blade shone with life. Under the great trees, heavy with leaf, little groups of people sat with picnics, each knot of humanity speaking a different language. The world had come together to relax in an English meadow, bounded by cliffs of tall, white stone. The air smelt of cava and sunscreen, with just a hint of urine from the bushes.

Over by the lake, ducks squabbled and splashed, the children of the water. Behind them on a shrub-covered island, pelicans surveyed the scene – masters of all since 1664. Visitors paid them tribute with camera flashes, which the pelicans acknowledged by furling and unfurling their huge white wings. I sat on the hot grass, letting the sun sober me up, smiling benevolently at everyone who passed. Big Ben chimed three. I got up, blessed the place and whistled all the way to the office.

It was debate day and June was determined that I should be prepared.

A double-spaced printout of my speech was on my desk, with key phrases to emphasise marked out in pink highlighter. June had placed an energy bar on one side, a packet of mints on the other. She watched me leafing through it, looking anxious.

I was still feeling the love. 'June, this is a triumph. Well done.'

She smiled, even blushed. 'Thank you, Robert. I did spend a lot of time writing it. It's a classic speech, a good speech – for a good idea.'

June had been an unexpected early convert to the tunnel idea, proclaiming it a 'common-sense policy with guts, proper politics'. I suspected that her sudden warming to me had more to do with the realisation that my political stock was rising, rather than a passion for tunnelling, but accepted it willingly. She had written the speech, briefed the journalists and cajoled some of her dinner party cronies to attend the debate.

With the Beaujolais, beef and bloat crowd on board, I knew it wasn't going to be a disaster. Adjournment debates are funny things – 20-minute affairs to round off the Parliamentary day. Backbenchers raise issues of great import to them, Ministers acknowledge that the issue exists, then everyone goes off to bed. Usually, their impact on the political agenda is one with the impact of Calpol upon typhoid. There are exceptions, however. Get enough MPs along to fill the backbenches, prod them into making supporting noises, pack out the public gallery and warm up the responding Minister, and you create the most elusive of things – a Parliamentary moment.

June had secured promises of attendance from 16 of the most sozzled and swollen – a very good attendance by adjournment standards. I had paid for Adam, his girlfriend and their assorted friends to come and watch proceedings, and for drinks beforehand to put them in an enthusiastic frame of mind. The Minister had been in touch with me in advance – an 11 pm phone call from an unknown number, an attempt to remember my name, a vague assurance that 'things were looking positive'.

Everything was coming together, everything was developing as planned. This was the day that would rocket the tunnel from idea to policy, and myself from obscurity to high regard and yet higher office.

I had asked Rachel to prepare two press releases: one a bog-standard account of the debate, and the other a paean of triumph should the Minister fully back the tunnel. I looked over both and told her to junk the standard. 'Confidence, Rachel, we must have confidence. He who dares wins.'

'Yes, sir. Did you want to go with 'delighted' or 'over the moon' in your quote?'

'Let's push the boat out, go for both.'

'So that would read, 'I am delighted and over the moon that the Minister has agreed to back the sensible, cost-effective and environment-saving plan to tunnel a new and shorter M17a route' – does that sound OK?'

'Excellent – actually, why not add an excellent in there as well? Just for good measure.'

It was fleeting, but I saw an eye roll in response. Rachael and I's relationship had continued to cool, just as Emily and I's had advanced.

'Will do. Oh, and sir – casework update for you. You know Mr Bradshaw over at Little Kingsley?'

'The man who sees Nazis everywhere?'

'That's the one. Well, he is in some trouble. Serious trouble. DWP have cut his pension in half, they have said they can't find his National Insurance records. He was in the Merchant Navy and he doesn't know what records were made.'

'Well, what I can do about it?'

'An urgent letter to DWP, asking for an exemption on compassionate grounds. A lot of chasing phone calls, and some meetings. It will be a lot of work, but I think we can do it.'

'Honestly, Rachel, not now. This evening is going to be the highlight of my career, I don't want brain space taken up by a scattery old loon who can't solve his own problems.'

It was odd, but I thought I heard a sudden growl.

'What did you say, Rachel?'

'Nothing.' Her cheeks were red from my rebuke.

And then, from somewhere, a whiff of pipe smoke.

The door opened. The arrival of Emily put the now-familiar smell, and all concern, out of my mind. She was flushed from laughter and looked like Spring incarnate, leading Adam and his friends in from a whirlwind tour of Parliament. Our office was at once full of people and excited chatter.

I played a good mein host, shaking every new arrival by the hand and learning every name. Adam's friends looked much like himself – sensible hair, earnest shirts, appropriate stubble. His girlfriend was the only woman among them, and gave me her usual firm handshake, with an extra squeeze to remind me that her articles for the South Gloucs Gazette could make or break the next election for me. Adam's eyes were shining and he burbled at me about how wonderful it was to be in Parliament, how at home he felt here. I slapped his back again and leaned in. 'Still no vacancies, matey.' It deflated him nicely.

I gave the assorted crowd a bright and breezy speech, telling them what an exciting moment this was for Holton, Netley and Pilford, and how proud my team should be at having got here. I thanked June, Emily, Rachel and Adam in turn, cheering up the latter two a little, and then ordered them all to the bar.

I resisted the urge to join them and went straight to the chamber. It always looks good to get there well before a speech you are going to give, feigning an interest in the business of the house as opposed to just your own moment in the spotlight. It meant I had to listen to two hours of discussion about shellfish harvest in Northern Ireland (a bumper crop this year, E. coli at moderate levels), then police budget estimates (price of rubber rising, due to rising sexual emancipation), and finally an urgent statement on the case of Rupert Mallinger-Smythe (hooray Henry in prison in Thailand, SAS to rescue following intervention from his house master at Winchester).

Normally I would have been sitting quaking on the green leather of the seats, but as afternoon turned into evening I felt calm. It was in part the lingering effect of the Arkell's Sunlight, partly the knowledge that a potent spirit was guiding my hand and guaranteeing my victory. June's speech nestled in my pocket, rustling with the promise of success. As the time for my debate drew nigh, June's pink-faced chums started waddling into the chamber, greeting me with greasy smiles. The public viewing gallery filled with Adam and his gang, and – blessed of blessings – Emily. I waved at her and she winked back.

The room was really filling up now, including a smattering of bright, ambitious young things. This was an excellent sign, suggesting that the whips were actively encouraging the keen to take part. One man who definitely hadn't been invited by the whips lurched by me in a bright yellow suit, smelling quite strongly of cherry brandy. Harry clapped a weak hand on my shoulder and whispered wetly that he was 'here to support'.

As Harry sat next to me with a squelch, the Speaker banged his gavel and uttered the words that had closed Parliamentary days since before the discovery of the potato: 'Motion made, and Question proposed, That this House do now adjourn.'

I was up.

I started with a classic formulation of delight at having the opportunity to raise an issue so close to 'my heart, and the hearts of my constituents', followed by a flash of ankle, 'and that goes – in a quite literal sense – to very heart of my constituency.'

I gave a potted history of the M17a proposals, from conception to stagnation, taking care to fulsomely praise the bravery my Party had displayed in committing to resolve the issue in its manifesto.

I dropped my voice an octave, and tuned to what 'tragically, looked set to be the inevitable cost of the road

– hundreds of acres of our precious, life-giving countryside'. To appreciative growls from the pink-faced men, I went into great detail about our green and pleasant land, and what the road plan would destroy for ever – 'the brook where the child plays, the meadow where the cow lays – the hedge that sheltered Saxon warriors and young lovers alike'. I went on in this vein for some time, like a demented National Trust guidebook, referencing Betjeman, Churchill, the tragedy of the commons and a fictional farming grandfather. 'He loved the land, and the land loved him. He would be turning in his grave, the one in the village churchyard, sheltered by the old elm, where the snowdrops bloom. But alas, the snowdrops now will be smothered in petrol fumes. And with them, the old man's heart.'

Harry uttered a sob. I hoped my real grandfather, a wicked old sod who had spent his life on the Bristol buses and his wages in the bookies, would forgive the forgery.

I dropped my voice still deeper, as deep as it could go. 'A terrible choice seems to confront us – to preserve the things we love, but halt progress – or to let progress rip, but to count the cost in the grain, oak and roses of old England.'

A sudden change of tone marked out by June in the speech script with a highlighted smiley face.

'I am delighted to be able to tell the house that this grim choice does not have to be made. We can – as the young people say – get us a plan that does both.'

A titter of laughter. On the benches in front of me, the back of the Minister's head moved in a mirthful way. Another excellent sign.

'I tell this house that we can build a tunnel. A tunnel to deliver the M17a road, relieve east–west and north–south congestion, and to preserve the green fields of Holton, Netley and Pilford. A tunnel at half the price of a full overground road.'

Harry shouted, 'A snip at half the price.' There was more laughter, albeit awkward and embarrassed laughter this time.

I flourished crumpled papers in my hand, Neville Chamberlain declaring peace-in-our-time style. 'These quotes are from a building company, showing how afford-able a tunnel would be – £10 million, as opposed to £21 million for the full road. It's a shorter route, you see, much shorter. With lovely firm West Country soil, firm but mal-leable. A tunnel, built by a reputable West Country build-ing company, is the better, cheaper option.'

Disregarding my father's grave-glare at calling old Cumgizzard a reputable builder, I pressed on. 'I do not blame my colleagues in government, or the civil servants who have looked at these plans, for failing to spot this opportunity. Sometimes it takes local knowledge – plus a bit of ingenuity – to cut the Gordian knot.'

I paused for a moment, to assume the amiable facial expression of a wise but modest man, blessed with ingenuity in spades. It was then technicalities for a few minutes, rattling through soil densities, moisture depths and bridging frames. Engineer impression done, it was time for the flatulent finish.

'A tunnel works for the ordinary, hardworking folk fam-ilies who live in Pilford and Netley, and the good people of Holton. A tunnel works for the lush green fields of England, and for the bright-eyed beasts that gallop so merrily on them. A tunnel works for the holiday makers who held joy-fully to the beaches of Devon and Cornwall, and for the lorry drivers who so dutifully hold open the arteries of trade that connects Bristol with the mighty steel pistons of the Midlands. A tunnel is a Great British idea, that will build a Great Britain. Let us build it together.'

There was a moment of silence. The lamps of the chamber flickered yellow, against the black night creeping in from the high windows. Aged, dusty stillness, like a tomb.

A clearing of ageing, overworked throats, a communal hawking. And then the most delicious of sounds – an affirmative hum. It rose from deep inside the cluttered bellies of the trenchermen, then mingled with the clearer, cleaner buzz of the bright young things, to soar sparkling to the public gallery to mix with the glass-muffled sound of applause. I gave a modest nod of the head, and sat down to soak every last precious drop of praise in.

It got even better. Normally adjournment debates pass swiftly from proposer to Minister – tennis ball to tennis bat, to home. This time, MP after MP rose to their feet to express their appreciation for thinking outside the box, for balancing the needs of nature with the economy, for building tunnels. I knew I had won when Tony Wellington, with an enamel poppy in his lapel (it was July), stood up to call for 'no more bureaucratic frippery – let's crack on with what is clearly a good idea. This is a chance for my honourable friends on the front bench to show that our Party is on the side of common sense, and good common-sense people.'

Cue another round of approving hums from the pink gentlemen in the back.

The Minister chuntered through seven paragraphs of standard fare – government funding for roads, government funding for petrol freezes, government funding to stop hedgehogs being squashed (a much smaller fund). She spoke of difficult decisions, of consultations, of stakeholders and all things. A first flash of substance: 'I am persuaded by the strong case my honourable friend has made for environmental protection and accept that building the M17a on the original proposed overground route would come at an unacceptable environmental cost'. Then, cloaked in sackcloth, came the shining beauty of the night. 'I am pleased to confirm that I have today commissioned a scoping study for the M17a relief tunnel.'

Cheers from the backbenches, cheers from the gallery. A wet handshake from Harry.

The house rose and I was engulfed in a wave of congratulations. It bore me from the chamber, through the Commons Lobby and into Central Lobby. Suddenly I was the most popular boy at school, hugely in demand. Jokes, handshakes, pinches in the ribs – even a warm smile and a thumbs up from Mary Miles.

Just as my face was beginning to tire from smiling and saying thank you, Tony took me by the arm and steered me away from the adoring mob.

'Let's have a chat, Robert. A proper one to one. Away from the throng.'

Making excuses on my behalf, and keeping my arm in a vice-like grip, Tony opened a small door behind a statue of Henry Writhosely-Evasine-Death (a 19th century Parliamentarian so forgotten that no one remembers how his name was pronounced) and propelled me down a flight of whitewashed stairs.

He opened a wooden door at the bottom with a small key, revealing a richer, warmer world.

'Welcome to Bellamy's, Robert. We'll be safe from the hoi polloi in here.'

Being inside Bellamy's had always been an ambition. On paper a Parliamentary bar open to all members, in reality a secret club only accessible to those who had the eye of favour on them. I had never been given a key, or even told where the bar was. It was everything I had hoped for – warm purple carpets, waiters in spotless white shirts, peanuts on little silver trays.

Tony directed me towards a window table, sheltered in its own dark wood booth.

'You will have champagne obviously – Demi Sec or Brut?'

There were different types of champagne? 'Your choice, Tony.'

'Jolly good – back in one tick. I have a dinner with the PM next week, and I want to run some ideas by you.'

I sat happily back in the chair and wallowed, a pig in the shit of power. The Thames ran like velvet under the window. On its other side, two lovers kissing on the Surrey shore, illuminated by lamplight. I was daydreaming about Emily when I felt motion on the other side of the table.

I turned, hand outstretched for the champagne glass.

'Getting waited on now are we, boy?'

It was, of course, him.

'I don't think this is the best time to catch up, Maurice. I have company.'

'Fear not, dear boy. Tony is flirting terribly with a waiter. We have plenty of time to talk.'

'Ok, well, can you be quick?'

'Oh yes, very quick. I came to congratulate you on a triumphant evening. You had them eating out of the palm of your hand by the end there. Very impressive.'

'Thank you.' I followed up with a smile, meant to close the conversation.

'Also to propose a thought.' Ah, fuck.

'You achieved a real shift in the government position tonight – for the first time they came out against building on the green fields. You have an opportunity now to put the whole project into touch. Drop the tunnel, they can't go back to the overground road. It can be over; you can end it.'

'But why would I do that?'

Something flickered across his limpid blue eyes. 'Boars Copse, which will have to go if the road comes, tunnel or no, is right in the path of either plan. It is a lovely bit of wood – some very old oak, a smattering of hazel. Good place for badgers also, one of the few remaining places for them in Pilford. It's the last bit of the Durden wood, which ran from my father's estate all the way to Avon.'

The flickering darkened, and the eyes became a fierce cobalt. 'You can force the government to scrap the road, on the environmental grounds they have admitted the value of. You can save the wood. Will you?'

I could not restrain a sigh of frustration. 'Look, Maurice, you have been really helpful, and I am grateful. But this tunnel is making my political career. I am not going to u-turn on it to save a few scrappy trees and a handful of mange-ridden, poxed-up badgers. Thank you again, but no.'

My phone started ringing. It was my mother.

'Shouldn't you get that?' Maurice's tone was oddly flat.

'No, she can wait.' I turned the phone off.

'My, we are very important now, aren't we. I heard there's an old sailor in Little Kingsley who needs your help. Are you too busy for him also?'

'Is this going to take much longer, Maurice? Tony will be back any minute.'

He rapped his hand on the panelling, twice in fast succession and then once more. It was an odd, deliberate gesture. Rationally it shouldn't have made any noise at all, the drumming of a dead man's empty fingers. Yet each rap sounded deep and heavy, like a bell tolling out over frozen fields, filling an empty winter sky.

Maurice got up, heavily. 'It is done. I shall see you at our constituency – at the Belvedere.'

With that, he dived out of the window, before I could ask him where or what the Belvedere was. He splashed into the Thames and glided fast, like a seal, upriver. To the west, and the setting sun.

Tony came back to the table, colour in his cheeks and a bucket of champagne in his arms. He poured me a glass, and held out his.

'A toast, Robert – to your career.'

Chapter 9

On my knees, I thanked God for all my recent success. I asked that my sins could be overlooked. I praised him for pouring out his – bounty? No, blessing. For pouring his blessings upon me. After that, I dried up and spent the next 30 seconds humming the tune of Lord of the Dance.

I was at the 'Netley Centre for Worship & Warmth' (formerly St Giles Church), following the injunction to prayer issued by a man who called himself 'the lead singer in the soul club' (formerly the vicar). Some form of thanks did seem to be appropriate, given the success of the debate and the subsequent two weeks. Seven excellent headlines, a well-done letter from the PM himself and, later that day, a ceremonial soil turning for the tunnel trial trench. Bliss was it in that dawn to be alive – to be noticed was very heaven. First, however, I had to endure the 'Friday Fun Fest' (formerly choral morningsong).

I tried to go along every few months or so. The Christian portion of my electorate, for all their talk of a brotherhood of man and cancellation of third-world debt, had proved very keen to vote Conservative as soon as I had expressed some coded concern about the 'decline of family life under this aggressively secular Labour government' (read gay people on TV, flavoured condoms in the gents and the Ann

Summers shop on Pilford High Street). To maintain their loyalty I grinned through church services on a semi-regular basis, picking the Netley Centre as the Church I was baptised in (back when it was called St Giles, and had a baptismal font as opposed to a 'paddle and praise pool').

The congregation loved the sense that I was 'one of their own' and, often in the past, the pervading atmosphere had struck a chord in me, although not the one intended. The room was always arid with frustration, from the tiny, tight shorts worn by the vicar to the glances of smothered, annihilated desire that flickered between members of the congregation, married and unmarried alike. When, as happened at least three times a service, people were incited to give each other a 'hug of peace', the smell of nervous, longing sweat rose and congealed under the shiny pine rafters. I had felt at home in this fellowship of confined, festering desire. Now, with Emily on my mind, I fantasised the readings, communal prayers and bad guitar playing away.

The vicar closed the morning's service by joining the 'Church band' in a rendition of Snow Patrol's Open your Eyes, putting his am round the teenage guitarist for the closing lines. It lingered there in the silence afterwards, for seven seconds too long.

Hanging on in quiet desperation, it's the English way.

Afterwards we gathered for a fraternal breakfast – stale croissants, cornflakes in Tupperware, metallic coffee. The chatter ranged from commendation (a kiss on EastEnders shown before the watershed), to speculation (as to the sexuality of the new owners of the Blue Anchor pub), to eager anticipation (of the fraternal lunch planned for later, and for the fraternal dinner planned for after that). When my cheeks started to hurt from grinning, and neck from nodding, I broke for a fag break. Usually, I stood and puffed alone on the steps of the church, but today I had company.

He was a small, older man, dressed – unlike the flock of youth leaders, lay pastors and soul shepherds I had left behind me – in clerical garb. His black cassock was frayed around the edges and his dog collar yellowing, in kinship with the fingers he had wrapped around a Dunhill cigarette. He nodded acknowledgement of my presence, and when my dying lighter gutted and failed in the breeze, offered me his.

'You want to be careful in there you know.' His accent was faded Indian subcontinent, stretched by years of Gloucestershire living and scratched by decades of Dunhills. 'Lot of people touched by the Holy Spirt. Very touched.' He tapped his yellow finger against the last of his hair.

I couldn't help but laugh.

'You know one of the churchwardens – sorry, soul shepherds, was telling me just now that he was writing a book about a sausage competition. Each chapter is told from the perspective of a different sausage. Isn't that the very mark of madness?'

I agreed it was and he suddenly cocked his head at me. 'Are you not our esteemed Member of Parliament? Mr, um, forgive me.'

'It is Wilkes. But call me Robert.'

He took my extended hand and shook it. 'I am Father Rahul. Honoured to meet you.'

'So, Father, what is it that brings you here – this doesn't seem like your congregation.'

'Good lord no. My church is up-country from here, deep in the fields. Same diocese. The Bishop – may his eminence be ever blessed – thought it might be useful for me to attend this [a wrinkle of the nose] centre of worship to learn a thing or two on reaching out to the young. How I am meant to apply this learning I do not know. The youngest person in my parish is 33. She is a horse.'

We laughed together, and then stood in companionable,

nicotine-suffused silence. My cigarette burnt out and, with a sigh, I tossed it away.

'Looks like it is time for me to return to the happy throng, Father. It was very nice to meet you.'

'And you.'

As I turned to leave, I felt his hand on my arm.

'Mr Wilkes, I do know one phrase that the young people use. We could – how is they say it? Ah yes – get out of here. How long do you have until your next bit of official business?'

'Just over an hour.'

'Well, you can spend that time listening to those good people talk about how marathon running keeps away the temptation of the flesh, or you can come and visit my church. A proper church. I'd hate for this morning to form your only view of the faith of the ancients.'

'I have to be outside Pilford at 12, and I don't drive. Thank you for the tempting offer, but I don't think I can.'

'This is resolved, nothing could be simpler. I have my car with me, I can drive you to my church, and then back to your appointment. All in good time.'

Sod it. I said yes. Father Rahul steered me back inside the centre, made some hurried excuses for me ('Mr Wilkes has to visit one of my parishioners. She is dying and wishes to see her member') and ushered me into his car. It was an old blue banger, smelling heavily of Dunhills, with a small statue of St Christopher stuck with Blu Tack on the dashboard.

We drove across Netley, through straggling industrial estates, past the waste grounds that formed the outermost spew of the city, and then out, deep into the countryside. As the July sun beat down upon the hedgerows, Father Rahul told me of his life – the childhood in the backstreets of Madras (I noted with interest that he did not call it by its modern name of Chennai), coming to manhood in a church orphanage there, the missionary work in China, the offer of an English curacy, then 30 years as Rector of Little Petherton. It was a tiny place, nestled in high hills, so out of the way that I had never leafletted it. We drew up before a honey-stoned church, surrounded by fields of yellow grain and green oak.

'Welcome to St Wulfric & King Charles the Martyr.'

Father Rahul anticipated my surprise. 'We are very loyal out here, Mr Wilkes. Wulfric was a local saint, for whom the church was named. After the English Civil War, the local people added the name of their murdered king, blessed be his memory. We still fast on the anniversary of his execution. Memories live long in these hills.'

The church door opened with a creak. There was a sense of movement inside the church, suddenly stopped, replaced by a watchful stillness. Father Rahul and I were the only people inside. The worship centre had smelled of pine air freshener and perspiration, but this church smelled as churches should – of beeswax, dying flowers, fading incense and dust. The pews were of dark wood, the walls a mouldering white. A set of skeleton-thin colours, from some long-abolished regiment, the green and white of the bell pull and the purple altar cloth, provided the only colour – along with one stained-glass window in the chancel wall. It showed a man in robe and sandals, feeding a bird of prey with grain from his open hand. An ill-looking pig watched the scene, his eyes picked out in sickly green glass.

'That's St Wulfric,' Father Rahul said. 'A missionary to the early kings of Wessex. He preached here, oh, about 15 centuries ago. Was very gentle apparently, kind to the birds and the beasts, made the buzzard lay down with the badger. They killed him of course.'

I made a noise of suitable sorrow and contrition.

'Come, if you are interested I have something else to show you.' He led me to a worn stone staircase recessed into a wall. After a short climb, he opened a door to dazzling light – we were on the roof of the Church tower.

The view was spectacular. The high grain fields around the church sloped away to the south, giving way to lush pastureland and then the suburbs of Bristol. At this distance, even Netley and Pilford had a certain dignity to them, backed by the church spires of the centre of the city, and behind them – just glimpsable – the high green of Mendip Hills. To the west, the Severn glinted as it wound its way to the sea.

Father Rahul pointed towards a spot of deep green, next to Pilford.

'That is the spot where St Wulfric was killed – beheaded on a hilltop on the orders of a pagan king. You see it is a wood? There is a folk tale that it didn't used to be, that the trees themselves sprung from the acorns that grieving birds brought to mark Wulfric's grave. There is an even stranger tale that a boar, one of the last of the princely wild boars of old, witnessed the killing and wept. The tears mixed with the blood and carried it to a brook, which bubbled from a spring just under the execution site. That brook feeds a stream, that becomes a river. The Thames to be precise. The old people say that is why the clay of the Thames is red – stained with the blood of a martyr, carried by the tears of a beast.'

'I thought the Thames rose in the Cotswolds?'

'That's the tourist board for you. No, it starts in that wood over there. Boars Copse is the name.'

Of course it was.

'I hear there are some plans or other for a road near there. Do you know anything about that, Mr Wilkes?' Father Rahul asked.

'Oh, there are always plans of some sort flying around. Can we go back inside? I am not too good with heights.'

I could have sworn that a look of disappointment flashed across Father's Rahul's face. In a second it was gone, and he was all smiles again, leading me down the tower steps and then conducting me round the various memorials embedded in the church walls. Farm boys killed on the Somme, various sons of the gentry killed in imperial adventures, Georgian squires killed by gout – all were remembered here, amid the ashy breath of summers past.

There was even a painting of the martyrdom of King Charles, made with heavy dark oils on dark wood. He looked Christlike, with his beady and gentle eyes, smiling as the axe came down.

Before I knew it, I was running late for my 12 o clock. I wrote my name in the visitors book (the person above me had visited in June 1991), dropped £5 in the donations box and let Father Rahul drive me, very fast this time, to Pilford. As I got out the car, thanking him profusely for his tour and the lift, he bid me to 'take good care, and care to be good. Care to be good, esteemed Mr Wilkes'. Then he was gone, in a cloud of exhaust fumes.

The welcoming committee awaited me. A crowd of local journalists, old Cumgizzard, a Bristol engineering firm and a clutch of assorted local worthies. Adam was there, talking intently to his reporter girlfriend. And there – just at the back – Emily. She winked at me then went back to chatting to a tall young man. He must be the Department of Transport Press Officer she had been tasked with escorting down from London. He was very tall, with broad shoulders. I pushed the familiar sinking feeling aside and reminded myself this was my day. The opening of the first test trench for the M17a tunnel, with me slicing the ceremonial sod and a government press release to be issued praising my role in delivering this 'sensible and sensitive investment in South West transport infrastructure'. And Emily was here. Truly, life was glittering.

The location was less so. We had gathered by a foot tunnel under the M5, suffused with the smell of urine and a decaying rat, its head fatally lodged in an empty can tossed by one of the drivers above. The faded slogan 'you've been Tangoed' was just discernible on the can's side. The rush of cars above us, alternating with the heavier thud of a passing lorry, created a vague sense of threat. In front of us stretched the footpath that marked the old railway line. It once had passed through fields, but now it passed through the outermost jettisoning of the city – a scrubby paddock or two containing unhappy-looking horses, storage yards bordered by savage iron fences, an industrial estate bordering a rubbish tip. Only one remnant of the former landscape remained: a beleaguered output of green trees on rising ground to our left. Boars Copse. The trees were closely clustered together, hunkered down in the face of the grey, steel and concrete that faced it, screening and guarding the open countryside that lay on the other side. It looked smaller than it had from the church tower.

Old Cumgizzard saw me looking at it. 'Spooky old wood that, lots of queer tales about it.'

'I just heard some of them,' I said, before pointing to a blur of stone above the treeline. 'What's that there?'

'Durden Belvedere. An old folly, built right in the heart of the wood. Lords and ladies used to take their tea there centuries ago. There's a spring at the bottom apparently.'

He took my strange look for something else. 'Don't worry, lad, I have already got the demolition order. The tower is going to go, along with the wood. That's where the tunnel spoil needs to be put. Can't stand in the way of progress, eh?' He winked hugely.

One of the journalists pulled at my arm. 'Are we good to start? We have to cover the jumble sale down at Bampton this afternoon.'

'Of course, my apologies. Ladies and gentlemen, gather round.'

I gave a short speech about new beginnings in old soil, and suggested – humbly of course – the new tunnel on the line on the old railway represented the return of pioneering Victorian values, of enterprise, of boldness, of imagination. I mused that only by tunnelling in line with the spirit of the past could we truly break through to the future. I concluded by showing the assorted cameramen the 'made in Bristol' stamp on the ceremonial shovel, bedecked with ribbons, and said we were both 'local boys, made good'.

Pause for laughter.

'On a serious note, though, I am proud that the labour and materials for this exciting trial phase will be provided by West Country companies. It will be proper handsome, as my dear father used to say.' Old Cumgizzard gave a seedy bow – the butler of a brothel, expecting a fat tip.

'I am hopeful that, if this trial finds the positive results that I expect it to, we can proceed to the full tunnel excavation that will create even more jobs, local jobs. Lovely local jobs for a lovely local tunnel. I am proud to support a government that recognises the value of the local, that has had the courage to back this exciting new chapter in the history of Pilford, and of glorious Gloucestershire. Ladies and gentlemen, friends – I give you, in honour of the past, the path to the future.'

I stuck the shovel into oozing ground. The cricket-click of seven cameras snapping all at once.

One of the cameramen suggested that I give it some welly. I was wearing brogues. The cameramen – all men, and blokey men at that – started to chuckle. To compensate

I started properly digging, prising forth great chunks of soil until I felt unexpected resistance. Something stretchy, but less yielding than the earth. A couple of further exploratory jabs and it was draped over the shovel.

Torn, stained, earth-covered y-fronts. Blue, with a white border.

The cricket-click of cameras started again. In panic I kept digging and felt more resistance under the shovel. For one horrid moment I thought of Crimewatch, of a pathologist's tent, grey-green flesh. The wrong type of big moment. An utterly ruined day. It was almost with relief that I saw another pair of underpants emerge from my excavation, black and lacy ones this time.

Excited chatter arose from the camera crowd. Old Cumgizzard loudly proclaimed that I had found 'a pervert's treasure-trove. The doggers love it round here'.

As the chatter turned into a gale of laughter and camera clicking approached frenzied proportions, the government press officer finally earnt his pay. He strode forward, hands outstretched – in the manner of press officers throughout the ages – and declared, 'That's a wrap, lads, you have all you need.'

It took ten minutes to usher them off and, by dint of threats and flattery, securing undertakings from them that they would only use the early photos.

Cue an afternoon of worry, until the evening editions came out – blissfully free of underwear. I looked quite distinguished in the snaps they used, sleeves rolled up, blue shovel ribbons matching my blue tie, a manly bead of sweat on my brow. The press officer had insisted on staying with me 'till we got the all clear' and – for want of anything better to do – we were in a bar, chosen as being the closest to Bristol Temple Meads and his train home.

The press officer did not seem keen to go. He was enjoying

the Foster's I had bought him, and the blush that came to Emily's cheeks when she had drunk too much. It was all very convivial, but – as an experienced third wheel myself – it was time for the fucker to leave.

'If you hurry, you can make the 9.39. Back in the smoke before you know it.'

'Ah, it's alright, there is no hurry, mate.'

I am not your bloody mate, you presumptuous little sod. 'I really think the 9.39 might be best. I'll get in trouble for keeping you here too late – overtime and all that.'

A very slow sip of his drink was his only answer.

'You'll miss the last tubes if you stay any later. I'll have hell to pay if you have to get a taxi. Very grateful for all your brilliant work today. I will be writing to the department to commend you.'

Honey always works. He got up and shrugged on his clearly expensive overcoat, looking to Emily to join him. She downed her glass of wine.

It may have been the relief coursing through me at the avoidance of the photo debacle, or the wine in my veins, but I suddenly felt brave. Maurice's voice rang in my ear. Decisive and manly action, that's the ticket.

'Actually, Emily, really sorry – I have got some urgent casework to go through with you. I might have to put you on the next train.'

Press officer started to open his mouth, clearly miffed at missing the opportunity of a shared tipsy train ride back.

I intervened before he could. 'It's ok, you live right next to Paddington, don't you, Emily? You'll be tucked up in bed before midnight, promise.'

'Sounds good to me, boss.' Emily settled back down in her chair.

I bundled press man out, before he could object further, with hearty thanks and a clap on the back.

Emily poured us both a fresh glass of wine. 'That was very brave, Mr Wilkes. Very bold.'

'Fortune favours the bold.'

'How fortunate do you expect to be?' She smiled, took a sip of wine and leant forward to whisper in my ear, conspiratorially. 'One might question your motivations. Dragging a young girl to your constituency and keeping her there, at the dead of night. What do you hope to achieve, Mr Wilkes?'

Her posh tipsy accent pronounced it Wulks. It was the sexiest thing I had ever heard.

'To show you the wonders of the South West and the delights of my constituency. And to widen your political education.'

'Educating me? How very exciting. And to go over the casework you mentioned, of course.'

Decisive, manly action.

'Yes, about that casework. It's very confidential. Might be best to go over it in more private surroundings. A hotel room perhaps.'

My suggestion lay heavily on the table between us, achingly vulnerable. Moments of agonising silence. She opened her mouth and closed it again. I prepared for a squashing.

Then she kissed me.

It was the work of moments to settle our bill, cross the street arm in arm, and secure a room at the Bristol Temple Meads Premier Inn. The receptionist seemed utterly disinterested in us, as did the other couple in the lift. No one knew who I was, and for the first time that knowledge was utterly delicious.

I will spare you the details of a dirty old man getting closer and closer to his heart's desire.

There was one moment of self-reflection, when Emily had popped into the bathroom to 'slip into something more comfortable'. I looked at myself in the mirror overlooking the bed, splayed on the purple and white Premier Inn duvet. The cheap wood varnish of the headboard, the utilitarian whiteness of the wall behind, the carboard cut-out of a purple hippo on the bedside table emblazoned with the message 'sleep like a dream'. My trousers and shirt, thrown over a trouser press. My shoes at the foot of the bed. These ordinary, dull things were sprinkled with magic – treasures from the world of faery, valuable beyond measure. One pathetic, glorious, teenage thought ran through my mind, again and again. In this room I was to become a man.

The bathroom door opened and Emily walked out, wearing nothing at all.

We were on the bed when the door knock came.

'Did you get room service you old romantic?'

'No. Did you?'

'Maybe they thought we were a newly married couple and have sent some champagne?'

I shrugged and went back to kissing her neck. The knock on the door came again.

'I better get your champagne, hadn't I?'

Emily gave a happy nod. I threw my shirt around my shoulders and padded to the door, opening it up just a crack so that only my top half could be seen.

The person behind the door pushed it open hard and I staggered back. There was a torrent of noise and movement. I recognised the click-click of a camera. Then Adam's face, looking stern. I was struggling to process his presence when I recognised his girlfriend, standing just behind him. Her hand was outstretched to mine, a recorder clasped in it.

'Mr Wilkes, can you confirm that Boar's Copse is in the ownership of your family? And that you stand to financially benefit from the tunnel project you have been promoting?'

Emily was screaming, scrambling under the covers.

'Mr Wilkes, is this girl a member of your staff?'

My belt and trousers fell off the trouser press, with a clatter like the end of the world.

Chapter 10

It was – as with so many other things in my life – my father's fault. Back in the late 80s he had managed to outdo even himself, by sleeping with my mother's best friend (Emeline, she of the orange hair and ten-a-day Dubonnet habit). As part of her conditions for staying, Mum had insisted on a new conservatory, a second blue Mini and the granting of a whimsical girlhood dream: a forest all of her own, for her to walk in wherever she wished. Dad, focused on the bottom line in business as in love, snapped up Boars Copse at a bargain-basement price – the scrappy, motorway-adjacent land on the less salubrious edge of the city could never be used for anything worthwhile. Mum got her wood, Dad avoided his divorce, and infant Robert – like so many other things in our colourfully wallpapered, heavily carpeted, secret-stuffed home – never got to hear about it.

Perhaps if we had had a mother–son relationship of any sort, I would have learnt of Boars Copse after my father died. Alas, my monthly payments to her and our yearly turkey and tension catch-ups didn't offer the sort of space to allow for the disclosure of whimsies like secretly owning a wood. She had tried to tell me, when the tunnel plan had hit the news. I had of course – following time-honoured precedent – ignored her calls. Giving up on my mobile, she had called the constituency office and got through to Adam. She had always been a sucker for polite young men and, without too much difficulty, he had coaxed her message from her, promising to pass it on.

Adam. Prigging fucking Adam. He had passed the message on, straight to his journalist girlfriend. His revenge on me for refusing to transfer him to London was to be absolute. They had both meant to confront me at the trench-cutting ceremony, asking about ownership in the very shadows of the wood itself. Then Adam had seen Emily's wink to me. His priggish spider senses tingling, he had delayed the moment of reckoning and followed me for the rest of the day. Emily and I's passage to the hotel room had confirmed things and – wallah – Götterdämmerung.

The rest of the night is something of a blur. Adam declaring that they 'had all the needed' and departing, chest puffed out in delighted outrage, Emily crying, pulling clothes on and running for the last train to London, the dead silence in the room after she had left. Whiskey ordered as room service, tasting bile, plans scrawled on the purple Premier Inn headed paper, plans discarded and flushed down the toilet to avoid discovery, a slap to pull myself together, a collapse into sobs. The sound of two drunks outside greeting the first rays of dawn with indecipherable yells. The music of my soul.

6 am and the tomb-cold light of early, early morning. The front page of the South Gloucs Gazette website updated.

'Holton MP in property and sex scandal'

A photo of me in the hotel room, eyes wide in surprise, open shirt failing to hide the flab, a modesty sticker at my crotch.

An investigation by the South Gloucs Gazette has sensationally revealed that the MP for Holton, Robert Wilkes, stands to benefit financially from the tunnel project he is backing.

Property ownership records show that Boars Copse, a wood due to be bulldozed to make room for the M17a relief tunnel, is owned by a very close family member*. The Gazette understands that the wood was valued at £20,000 at the start of the year. The Department for Transport has now purchased the wood, to allow for tunnel exploration works at their standard project rate of £5,000 per acre, coming to a total of £80,000.

When the Gazette went to put these questions to Mr Wilkes, we found him in a hotel room with a junior member of his staff. Miss Emily Harvey-Batten, who is thought to be under the age of 21, was naked and Mr Wilkes was in a state of partial undress. Mr Wilkes was in a state of heightened excitement, such that he could not answer our questions. We have asked the Conservative Party for comment.

*Sadly, the only inaccuracy in the whole article.

I stopped scrolling, to be copiously sick. The room stank of sweat and vomit and seemed to be shrinking. In one corner, one of Emily's socks sat, forgotten in the rush. It was a blue pop sock, nothing remarkable, but in its colour and softness seemed to represent all I had lost, in the eternity between arriving in the room and now.

I had to get out. Stumbling past the thankfully unstaffed reception, blinking in the light of the street, deafened by seagulls squawking with a deranged loudness. Shelter in a taxi, one of the ones where the driver is mercifully mute and the radio covers the silence. As we drove out of Bristol, the most exquisite of the tortures of the condemned man began – an irrational sense of hope. Radio 2 was full of an EU conference, an earthquake in Peru and a new England manager. I wasn't mentioned at all. Perhaps this would just be a little local difficulty? The South Gloucs Gazette was just a local rag, doomed to a declining, elderly readership and an increasing proportion of ads. The short walk from Holton taxi rank to my flat provided further encouragement – the joggers, cleaners and shopworkers who populated the 7 am streets showed no sign of any special recognition or interest in me.

By the time I reached my first door I had resolved on a winning plan of action. A damning correction (content TBC), to be backed by legal threats and published in the Gazette the very next day, redundancy for Adam (maybe a harassment charge as well), flowers for Emily. I half-remembered a quote from some be-medalled general facing disaster in one of the World Wars – 'My centre is yielding. My right is retreating. Situation excellent. I attack' – and wandered round the flat, repeating it and waving my fist for emphasis. I was going to come through this stronger. I had a ghost on my side for fuck's sake. This was probably all part of his plan. I left a voicemail for Google's top result for defamation lawyer and went to wash the vomit off my face.

The phone rang just as I got out of the shower.

'Hello you naughty boy.'

'Who is this?'

'Sadly for you, not a teenager. It's Mary. Mary Miles.'

Hope curdled into a small lump, curled in the depth of my stomach.

'Mary, let me explain. I know this all must look very bad, but…'

'I have zero interest in listening to you wriggle around and to try and explain things. Let's spare me, and you, the horror of going over your pathetic little perversions and horrid little schemes. Brass tacks time.'

Black mould spread over the little ball of hope. I stuttered down the phone.

'You will be leaving Parliament. It is your choice as to how you leave.'

'Leave?'

'My, you are a quick learner. There are two types of

leaving. You can resign straight away, with apologies for the disgrace you have brought to the Party, and disappear out of sight. Like a stone down a well. I strongly recommend this course to you.'

A little bubble of defiance popped out. 'You can't make me resign, can you? Besides, you don't want a by-election, you would lose it.'

'That's all taken care of, and you don't need to worry your pretty head over it. As to your question, that brings us to the second type of leaving. You could choose not to resign.'

'I am not going to resi-'

'A choice not to resign would be very brave, Robert. We will condemn you utterly; why, the PM might even have to learn your name to say how abhorrent you are. We will withdraw the whip, and you will sit friendless and alone. We will encourage every journalist to dig into your past, your proclivities, your internet history. Years of bad headlines, of being a public stain on Parliament. And then, like an owl putting a dying mouse out of its misery one moonless night, we will deselect you as soon as an election comes. One big gulp. Gone.' The smacking of her lips was audible, even down the phone.

'Oh, and Robert – the girl. If you care about her at all, go now. She can be forgotten if you are, or hauled over the coals with you if you decide to linger for a basting. Your choice.'

'How long do I have?'

'Decide by 6 pm today. The current line is that we are looking into the allegations, it will hold for the day. Choose wisely, Robert. Go now and be forgotten, or stay and be reviled – and then go anyway.'

She put the phone down.

One thought cut through the bedlam of fear, confusion and sleep deprivation. Maurice. Maurice would know what to do.

How to contact him? How do you contact a ghost? I thought of praying, but it seemed blasphemous. I called his name. Nothing. I called a little louder. I felt ridiculous.

I wrote his name down on a piece of paper and burnt it with a cigarette lighter. It curled into ash and the room smelt of chemicals. No large, bristling figure conjured itself before me.

I looked for the oldest thing in my flat and decided on the poker that I had inherited from the previous owner, a rusted hunk of old metal with a brass knob that suggested a Victorian origin. I grasped it, screwed my eyes shut and tried to think of the past. Flat caps. Cobbles. The smell of rain on tweed. Horse manure. Woodsmoke.

I opened my eyes. My stained sofa, small television and framed poster of John Wayne (also inherited from the previous occupant) was all that there was to see.

One final, despairing, mad idea. I subscribed to a family history website, one of the big ones where people disappointed with their own lives can lose themselves in someone else's. They had telephone directories dating back decades, long scanned lists of names and phone numbers, junk information preserved for eternity in the lumber room of online. I typed his name and within a matter of moments I found it, in a list from 1954:

The Hon Maurice Copeland-Ellis MP. 3 Lantern Court, Pimlico.

Chelsea 362-699

It must have been his London home. I typed the six numbers into the mobile, spelling Chelsea out with the touch-pad numbers. I held the phone to my ear, expecting silence.

There was instead three long beeps. A burst of white noise. Three further beeps, more muffled this time – as if they came from far away.

'Hello, Robert.'

'Maurice?'

'The very same.'

'Good God, I can't believe that worked. Um, Maurice, something has happened. I need to sp-'

'Yes, of course you do. We will meet. Come to Boars Copse at 11. Walk until you hit the tower.'

I looked at my watch. It was already 10.

'Is that a bit early, Maurice? You are in London aren't you? We can make it later.'

'I am speaking to you from beyond the grave, Robert. I can make it. See you at 11.'

Another beep and the phone went dead. Clothes, shave, chewing gum, a conscious effort to push Maurice's cold tone to the back of my mind, another taxi, another mercifully mute driver, 13 calls from journalists on withheld numbers, 4 from constituents shouting abuse, phone turned off, 5-minute walk over allotments and waste ground – and then, the green of the wood.

It was so very green that summer morning. All the trees were in full bloom and, as soon as I went a few steps into the wood, the rush of the motorway stopped, as if screened out. Unlike the waste ground on its margin, the earth in the wood was free of litter, the brown soil exhaling a warm, heavy air that mixed with the spice rising from the tree bark. Although I could see no other animal or person, there was an air of movement, a breezing, whirling presence just out of sight.

I walked on, as if guided by the breeze, until the trees began to thin out and the sky opened up. Before me was a stretch of lawn, a good English, manicured lawn, sitting perfectly and preposterously in the middle of this wildwood. A small stream ran through the grass gin-clear, with green clusters of weed swaying in its waters. The stream climbed up a hill, and the lawn with it, until just before the top it disappeared under a tottering building of brown brick. It had a great central block, with window spaces open to the sky, flanked by a tower, topped with crenelations. Durden Belvedere.

I wondered how often my mother had come to this place and felt an unexpected stab of admiration. What a kingdom to own, visit and keep as a perfect secret. Had she mown this grass? Had she kept the river clean?

A voice broke me out of my reverie.

'Come up. Further up and further in.'

It was Maurice's voice. Looking up I saw his outline at the top of the tower.

I walked up the hill, sweating in the sun, and pushed open the oaken door of the Belvedere. The smell of abandonment, of spider webs built on the dust of a thousand predecessors, the mildew of a century of winters, of dark, dank, waiting coolness, greeted me. Walking forward using the light of my phone, narrowly avoiding stumbling over a rotting croquet set, I became aware of another thinner light to my left. I ducked under a low arch, to see a group of men and women crouched at a card table. The men wore brocaded coats, knee britches and white lace cravats, the women high wigs and robes of silk. Candles flickered in the gloom. They turned and looked at me, their faces pale, cards grasped tightly in their hands. One of the men raised his eyebrow, and with the jerky movements of a marionette long unused to motion, bowed low and gestured for me to join the game. A small brown mouse ran across his alabaster face.

I ran, back into the dark and out of the frail, unearthly candlelight and straight into a set of stairs. Sweating all the more, clinging onto the reassuring blue, modern light from my phone, I climbed higher and higher, away from the horror beneath me. The sunlight when at the top was hugely welcome, as was the bulky form of Maurice, standing with his back to me looking out over the battlements. I went to join him. The view from the top was not quite as expected. There was the stream and lawn below, and the wood all around it, but beyond that there were no buildings, no roads glistening like white snakes across the land. Instead, there was green, as far as the eye could see – rolling, deep green, cut through only with the blue of the Bristol Channel to the west and to the east, the long blue line of a river, almost turquoise in the sun.

Maurice grunted acknowledgement of my presence, but said nothing more. He stayed silent, looking out at the view.

'Maurice, why can't I see any houses? What is this place?'

Silence.

'Maurice, I need your help.'

Still nothing.

'I really need your help. You know what happened, don't you?'

He turned round, and his face was terrible. Eyes black, moustache quivering, nostrils flaring. 'Yes, I know what happened. You followed your greed for power, and ignored every other call, every duty.'

He yelled the word 'duty', in a voice hoarse and deafeningly loud. I felt fear then, with a sudden awareness of the reality that Maurice was not an adviser and friend. He was a dead man, haunting me.

'I am sorry, I am really, really sorry. But I thought you wanted to help me, to get me to Cabinet. So I can deliver for Holton.'

'You are not at a fucking hustings now, Wilkes. You don't need to pretend. If you say 'deliver' one more time, or mention 'change', or 'common sense', I will eviscerate you, I have known what you are from the start, I was watching you from the moment you got elected. We have been watching you.'

A shiver down the spine. I turned round, away from the view. The space between me and the staircase was now filled with people. Men in old-fashioned suits, men in evening dress, men in brocade coats like the players downstairs, men in cloaks with swords at their sides, men in armour with hunting dogs at their feet – medieval tomb effigies come to life. I started to recognise faces, including the one woman there – wasn't that Jean, MP for Holton in the late 70s? And next to her, looking disapproving, yes it was him. Dr Duncan Middleton, the man I had defeated for the seat in 2010. He was still wearing the battered Labour rosette that all Labour candidates had borne into battle in Holton since the First World War.

Maurice walked over to join them, turning to face me full-on. 'We see you, Robert Wilkes. We know you. We know you as a coward, as a knave, as a disgusting little worm of a man.'

'Look, Maurice, that's hardly fair. I have worked ha-'

'We have seen your work, boy. Self-gratification, self-promotion, selling the land you were meant to protect.'

One last ebb of defiance. 'But the tunnel, it was all your idea. You told me to go for it with Emily as well. This was all you, it's not my fault.'

'I laid out some options for you, and you went for them, like a pig snuffling after truffles. You see, we knew very early on that you didn't care about Holton, its places and people, only for yourself. We put temptation before you, knowing you would fall to it, and utterly destroy yourself. We knew you would succumb, and Holton would be better off for it. Better off without you.'

'So it was a trap?'

There was a hint of the old twinkle in Maurice's eye. 'I did give you a way out. Remember back in Bellamy's? I suggested you drop the tunnel and save the wood. You declined your redemption. I also advised you to speak to your mother. A chap should always speak to his mother. Father Rahul also tried, only yesterday, one last time. He is a kind soul, but mistaken to think you would listen. Three chances, three turnings away. Three turnings away from the good. Why, you even refused to help that poor old sailor in Little Kingsley, bereft and in need of aid. You failed to hear the call to good, even when I growled it in your ear. The land sang to you, but you shut up your heart.'

I thought of bolting, out down the stairs and away. My way was entirely blocked by the spectral, waiting crowd. I looked through it, seeking an avenue of escape. There was a gap on the left, filled only by a man in a simple brown robe and sandals. He seemed fainter somehow than the others, as if standing further away. I dashed forward towards him, praying that my elbow would move him aside. Suddenly from behind his legs a huge, growling boar moved forward to bar my path, massive head down, tusks jutting forward, eyes blazing with hate. I retreated.

Maurice smiled. 'You recognise old Wulfric I presume – and his faithful friend? We have been watching over this wood for a long time, some of us for a very long time indeed.'

'Why are you doing this to me?' I noticed the sob rising in my voice and tried to push it down.

'What's it all for?'

He started to fill his pipe, talking all the time. 'You know, I studied Anglo-Saxon poetry a bit, when I was up at Oxford, before the War. One phrase always stuck with me – wraithlike is our native stone. We are the wraiths guarding this native stone, becoming one with it as our long watch winds on. The native stone that gives all life and whose beauty inspires the living to good deeds. It is the message scrawled in the sand.'

He breathed a great belch of tobacco into my face. 'And

we can't let little shits like you rub the message out, all for the sake of a few extra scraps of self-worth to fill the void inside your chest. Cutting down Boars Copse, destroying the last remnants of the great Durden wood. Pah! A sacred place, one of the most sacred places in this sacred England. Where holy blood stained the Thames, where the river gives breath to the land and hope to its people. Where I played as a boy. Where I met my wife over croquet. You would not defend this place, or a hundred others in this constituency. In just the same way, you would not defend its people. The shame of it!'

Like a ghastly House of Commons on a day of scandal, the assembled ghosts started bellowing 'Shame! Shame! Shame!'

Maurice pointed his finger at me, and I had a sickening feeling that his denunciation was reaching its climax. 'You are undone, Robert Wilkes; the pit closes over you. Your sin, your failure to protect the green places, has fittingly become the engine of your destruction. You will no longer be MP for this sacred place in a sacred land – and the land and its people will be better for it. There will be no tunnel, no road. We will protect our native stone. We, the MPs and guardians of Holton, condemn you. Be cast out and be forgotten.'

As one, the former MPs for Holton stepped forward. As they advanced, I saw strange creatures at their back, behind the knights, behind even Wulfric. They looked like men, but also like trees, and rocks, even flowers. One, with long willow-like leaves sweeping the floor, was wearing what appeared to be a Roman Centurion's helmet. I fell back before all of them, frantically grasping the battlement, hanging on to the reality of the warm stone. My predecessors kept advancing, until they were all around me. A feeling like plunging into heart-stopping water. Hands, gripping me, lifting me aloft.

I felt one hand tugging at my head and recognised a voice I had last heard on the campaign trail. Duncan Middleton whispered, dead into my ear, 'If you ever so much as stand in the same room as one of my daughters, I will teach you what it is to scream.'

The hands lifted me higher, above the battlements. The sun shone above me, huge, white and pale. For a few long moments I was suspended, limbs splayed. Visions of sacrifices on top of Aztec temples, torn skin, savage gods. There was an obscenity in the contrast between the heat above me, burning into my face, and the ice-cold hands beneath, the dead fingers digging, gouging into my back. Then a chant, deep, guttural, ancient, from a time of raging sea, ice on the river and wolves in the wood: 'Out. Out. Out.'

Sudden, sickening, plummeting motion. The world turning over and over, one last glimpse of the top of Belvedere, rapidly falling up from me. There seemed to be no one on it. Before I could look properly, my body turned again, facing the ground. The wind and my howl joined into one conjoined horror.

Grass, the soil underneath it, the deep stone at its core. Native, knowing stone rising to smash and scatter.

And then, like rain stopping play, sudden drenching water. The brook stretched out an arm and claimed me, scooping me up and into it. Here all reason leaves me, and nearly all description. The river carried me far from the hard, merciless ground, to grottos beneath the water, to caves deep under time. There, by a fountain that glittered like diamonds on a wall of rock, stalagmites and fossils of creatures beyond reckoning, I saw the Lady of the River, in a cloak of kingfishers. Up and away the birds flew, bearing me and her with them, to a distant stretch of the river and a starless night. She slipped out of the cloak and I saw at once a boy, playing a pipe amid the reeds. A silver light curled upwards towards the sky, warming the air. A dawn rose to meet it, at first pink then a bursting yellow, and into that dawn my friend flew, a swan now, every slow, heavy flap of wings an eternity of joy. I sank into the red mud of the river, giddy and hot in the new light, and felt the morning take its first, deep breath. Woods bowing to drink. Far downstream, London beginning with a gasp. A thousand beautiful, heart-filling, life-giving songs, etched in the blue sky, swirling in the green river. The river. The river. The river.

I came to next to a sewer pipe. A group of children from Pilford Grange School (maroon uniforms, £3,000 a term, city-leading teenage pregnancy rates) were perched on a dying willow above me, smoking. One of them was holding my phone, another rifling through my wallet. I retrieved both items with all the dignity a man in a soaked suit can muster and sloshed my way out of the stream. One of the children threw a bottle of Irn-Bru. It bounced off the back off my head, and came to land next to a discarded barbecue, with a dead pigeon draped across it.

I climbed away from the stream, the roar of the M5 around me. The road lay a hundred metres away, across waste ground. Behind me, up the stream, lay the Copse.

1 pm. Seventeen missed calls. I called Mary to resign.

Epilogue

Mary and the Party had my resignation fully taken care of, courtesy of Adam. The sanctimonious little shit was the designated successor, lauded by the Party Chairman within two hours of my hara-kiri as a 'brave public servant, who put the interests of his country before that of his employer'. Selected as the Conservative candidate a week later, elected a month after that.

The bastard got his move to London, got my seat in the Commons, got my office, got my staff. Well, June at least. She stayed on, delighting in her new title of Chief of Staff. Rachel – bless her gentle heart – moved on to a civil service role, 'away from all the unpleasantness'. She sent me a card expressing sympathy, with a guilty-looking puppy on the cover. Emily did not get in touch. After 12 calls, 37 texts and 4 bunches of flowers I received a short, curt note from her father saying that she had gone travelling and would be uncontactable on a game reserve in Kenya for the next 6 months.

She probably could have come back sooner. We both faded away from the headlines pretty quickly, after an initial rash of coverage in the tabloids (the photo of me at the door made it to two front covers). We were a campaign talking point for a few weeks, and then a cheeky footnote to Adam's election. Adam's maiden speech (piss and treacle, layered around an announcement that he would donate 10% of his salary to a charity supporting whistle-blowers) saw one last article mentioning my name, and then the water of oblivion closed around me. I was forgotten. Mary was right.

Severance pay and the sale of my flat in Holton could only keep me in Asda own-brand gin for so long, and I got a job in a Bristol trainer shop, renting a tiny box room nearby. Days drifted by in a haze of overbright light, leather fumes and scratchy branded t-shirts. The anonymity was comforting at first, but after a while I found the artificial, plastic world around me nauseating. I began to crave older, kinder things. I started eating my sandwich lunch every day in an old churchyard, marooned between two roads and the mall's goods yard, lingering between the old stones (you may not be surprised to learn that my search for St Wulfric's & King Charles the Martyr led to a long derelict, roofless channel and Father Rahul's moss-covered grave in the churchyard). I volunteered at Bristol Museum on Saturdays, where the old dears who it ran valiantly pretended not to know who I had been. Catching the bug for gentle things and gentle people, my Monday evenings were dedicated to volunteering at the Bristol food bank. I even began to take tea at my mother's, blood-sugaring over my initial awkwardness with carrot cake.

Thus it was that when a position came up as the caretaker of an abandoned great house, I applied with enthusiasm, and rejoiced when I was accepted. The place, Morduant Hall, was old, a great crumbling mass of honeyed stone, in the southern, Somerset-facing part of Bristol. It had been built by one of the city's merchant princes as a country villa, before being engulfed by 1930s suburbs, taxed into abandonment in the 40s, and taken over by the city council in the 50s. It had served as a teacher training school, then a children's home, before the inevitable scandal had forced closure. The stain of scandal still hung over the place, and now the council left it empty, an embarrassing name, kept out of sight. It was perfect for me.

My duties were janitorial and light, keeping the place ticking over, holding the mice at bay. I walked the long echoing corridors, day after day, lost in reveries of what had been. The balls, in a blaze of candlelight and violin, the hunting parties and the smell of wet dog in the hall, the port and cigar smoke lingering from the cold November night in 1812 when the Prince Regent visited on his way to Bath. I drank cups of hot sweet tea in what used to the main dining room and kept my scant supplies of tools (one torch, one spanner, one baton in case of intruders) on top of the magnificent fireplace that had somehow survived the depredations of the 20th century. Vine leaves curled upwards in marble, shrouding satyrs and fawns, engaged in an eternal bacchanal. A bored child had drawn a moustache on the central satyr, in some form of permanent marker that I could not scrub off, along with the immortal words 'Biffy is a shithead'.

A year passed, blank at first, then content, then happy. It was a late summer, when the leaves of the oak by the gate were turning powdery in the sun, that the delegation came. The West of England Local Development Partnership had decided to bless Morduant Hall with its honeyed touch, and had signed a deal whereby, in exchange for new flats replacing the oak and the slumbering ponds beside it, a developer would 'regenerate' the building into offices – its own regional HQ. The deal had a good write-up in the Bristol Mail (four new jobs created, eyesore removed) and now the men in suits were coming for a commemorative handshake and photograph. Assorted CEOs, growth directors, aldermen and MPs walked their brogues purposefully along the floors I had specially polished for the occasion, slapping backs and swinging dicks.

I spent most of the day hiding in my dining room cubby hole, searching on my phone for a new caretaker role. It had been made very clear to me that the new, shiny future for Morduant Hall did not have me in it. Besides, I had seen the cast list for the delegation, and it had Adam on it. Adam had carved out a lucrative regional development niche, stamping his name on every infrastructure project from Weston-Super-Mare to Worcester. He had been given a post as Parliamentary Private Secretary to the Secretary of State for Business, Innovation and Skills, and had – in part payment – recently come on the record to champion the M17a relief road, and to argue that it should proceed as originally planned, overground. The general consensus seemed to be that was a wise move, putting a scandal-drenched subject to bed with a clear, strong decision. As Adam said in the Commons, while 'environmental concerns required acknowledgement', 'the last word has to be three – jobs, jobs, jobs'. This was 'a bullet that had to bite', the Bristol–Birmingham sub-region needed 'direct action to unblock the arteries of commerce'. A bright future signing off on government press releases beckoned for Adam.

I was on my fourth cup of tea, straining my ears to detect whether the booming laughter from the press conference outside had taken on an octave of farewell, when I noticed a smell that I had tried but failed to forget. Pipe smoke. I turned to its apparent source, the old marble fireplace, to see a thin stream of blue-grey smoke emitting from the defaced satyr. Then there was a clunking, from somewhere deep in the chimney, and guffs of smoke from the empty fireplace itself, as if some phantom fire was raging. Then a whistle, growing louder, like a train approaching a tunnel. The cloud from the fireplace became bigger, bellowing out in great curls of spice and nicotine. The cloud took on a familiar shape, forming a face with a commanding nose and a bristling moustache, followed by broad shoulders and a broader waist. Like a bear emerging from his hibernation cave, Maurice stepped out of the fireplace. The whistle stopped.

It was expected somehow. I nodded in greeting.

He smiled, in a way that he had when first he had come striding into my life.

'Hope you are behaving yourself, boy. I have some business to be about.'

With that, he seized the spanner that sat on top on the mantlepiece and walked over to the window. He stopped to sniff the air and turned round to me. 'A fine old place this. Fitting place for tragedy. Bite the bullet indeed. Pah! I'll show him direct action.'

He swung the spanner, in an experimental fashion. 'Turns out that shit Adam is a treasonous shit. And a clever shit, much cleverer than you were. Got to be a bit more direct this time. Worth a try, skull might crack like an egg. He'll be laid up for a bit at the very least.'

'Maurice?'

'Yes?'

'There are wire cutters in the shed by the pond.'

Comprehension dawned, followed by a smile. 'We will make something of you yet.'

With that he chuckled and slid out of the window. I watched him run over to the shed, and then to the gravelled drive to where the VIP cars waited for their passengers. He ducked under one and was lost to my sight.

Fifteen minutes later there was the sounds of engines revving and a crunch of gravel. A minute or so after that, further away but distinct in its violence, came the squeal of brakes, the shriek of tyres and a heavy thud.

The Prime Minister attended Adam's funeral. Boars Copse stands still. My mother and I visit it sometimes, and feel quite content.